The Scarred Heart

Denise Patrick

Samhain Publishing, Ltd.
11821 Mason Montgomery Road, 4B
Cincinnati, OH 45249
www.samhainpublishing.com

The Scarred Heart
Copyright © 2013 by Denise Patrick
Print ISBN: 978-1-60928-940-9
Digital ISBN: 978-1-60928-873-0

Editing by Sue Ellen Gower
Cover by Scott Carpenter

First Samhain Publishing, Ltd. electronic publication: April 2012
First Samhain Publishing, Ltd. print publication: March 2013

Look for these titles by
Denise Patrick

Now Available:

The Importance of Almack's
Family Scandals
Love for Christmas
The Scarred Heir

Gypsy Legacy
The Marquis
The Duke
The Earl

Praise for Denise Patrick's
The Scarred Heart

"This quick and satisfying Regency romance...is mired in pain and suffering, redemption and love—and all the complexities therein. Fans of Regencies will welcome this addition to the genre, as will anyone searching for a great historical love story."

~ *Library Journal*

"*The Scarred Heart* was a thoroughly entertaining read that made you want to get to the bottom of the mystery involving these sweethearts."

~ *Joyfully Reviewed*

Dedication

To Chelsea and Sam and their Happily Ever After. I love you both.

Prologue

Westmorland County, England
May 1815

In a brightly appointed bedroom, the midwife had finished bathing the newborn while the maids helped the mother. As soon as all was clean, she approached the bed. The older woman sitting beside the new mother reached for the infant.

"Look how beautiful she is," she crooned softly to the mother. "What will you name her?"

From the bed came no answer. A small cry from within the blanket caused the older woman to look up. "Did you find a wet nurse?"

"Yes, m'lady, but I thought the young missus would want to feed the babe herself like she did the last one." She glanced at the young woman in the bed who appeared to be asleep. Red-gold curls had been tamed back into a long braid, but the young woman was extremely pale. Worried, the midwife reached over and touched the young woman's face, relieved to discover no fever. "Is ye all right, ma'am?"

The young woman turned away, and it was then that the midwife noticed the tears. They leaked from beneath dark lashes, sliding silently into the hair at her temples. The older woman got to her feet as the child began to cry in earnest. "Where is she?"

The midwife turned from her puzzled scrutiny of the mother. "In the sitting room, m'lady." She crossed the room to the door of the sitting room, only pausing momentarily to look back at the figure in the bed before she led the woman and child through the door.

As she introduced the woman she'd found to nurse the child, she wondered at the strangeness of this birth. Three years ago, the same young woman had delivered a healthy baby boy and had been so happy she refused to employ a wet nurse. Perhaps the rumors she'd heard in the village had some truth to them after all.

Still, the mother was young—only nineteen. Perhaps she no longer considered having small children the blessing she'd thought it at sixteen. Or she just needed to rest. Even though it hadn't been a difficult birth, the labor only lasting a few hours, it had still been hard. A good night's sleep would help everyone and, for now, the babe was well taken care of. The young woman she'd engaged would see the child was well nourished.

Yet, as she watched the grandmother fuss over the infant, she wondered what the future would bring for the child if her suspicions turned out to be true. A child who was unwanted by its own mother.

Chapter One

Essex County, England
November 1820

The heavy thump of McKeown Manor's door knocker forced Emma Laughlin's attention from her mending. Moments later, the drawing room door opened to admit a stylishly dressed young woman.

"Lady Royden to see you, madam."

"Sarah!" She jumped to her feet, the garment swiftly laid aside. "What brings you out on such a dreary day? Graves, tea for our guest, if you please."

The butler withdrew and she embraced her friend.

"You are looking better every day. How are you feeling?"

Lady Royden laughed. "I am fine." Taking one of the padded chairs, she brushed a stray lock of pale hair from her face. "Between you and Max, I can barely take two steps without someone coming to my aid. I am not made of porcelain."

"Yes, I know. Unfortunately you look as though you are."

"If this is what the next few months will be like, I may have to shoot Max to put him out of his misery."

"Be thankful you aren't sixteen."

The door opened to admit Mrs. Smythe carrying a tray on which rested a gleaming silver tea service. Placing it on the small table before Emma, she smiled at Emma's thanks before leaving and closing the door behind her.

"Ah, a hot cup of tea will be just the thing," Sarah said.

Once they were settled with their cups, Emma looked over at her friend. "So, to what do I owe this visit?"

"I've come to formally ask you to be David's godmother. We will be holding a small house party for his christening next week."

Surprise kept Emma immobile for a few seconds. "Me?" she finally managed. "You want me to be your son's godmother?"

"Of course," was the response. "Max and I have talked it over." She leaned forward and put her cup and saucer down on the tray. "Please say you will. I can think of no one I'd love more to be my baby's godmother."

Emma didn't know why she was surprised. From the first day she met Lady Royden nearly a year ago in the small village of Calder's Cross, they seemed to hit it off instantly. Newly married and in mourning for her brother-in-law, Sarah still made the effort to make the acquaintance of those living around Calderbrooke, the country seat of the earls of Calderbrooke. McKeown Manor wasn't large, but it was comfortably situated on a few acres of beautiful parkland abutting the southern end of the estate. Emma had been living there quietly for almost three years before she'd met Sarah.

Viscount and Lady Royden had accepted her as Emma Laughlin, widow, with a young son, Jamie. She'd been granted permission by her brother, the Earl of Englevyn, to live at McKeown Manor as long as she and Jamie needed. For now, that was all they knew about her.

Smiling with difficulty, she looked across at the vivacious

viscountess. "Very well. I'd be honored."

Sarah clapped her hands. "Wonderful. Now, would you mind very much if we wanted you to come up to Calderbrooke to stay for the house party?"

Her smile dimmed. "I don't know. What would I do with Jamie?"

"I would say you should bring him with you, but somehow I don't think an eight-year-old would have much fun with all the adults around."

She shook her head. "No." She took the time to replenish her cup from the pot while she thought. "I could ask Mrs. Wight if Jamie could stay with her for a few days. He and Abel are such good friends, I don't think it would be a problem."

"Perfect."

"I'll have to see if I have anything to wear that's not too out of date."

"You must wear that beautiful green velvet you made for last Christmas. It does wonders for you. Even Max remarked that you looked lovely."

And that was a compliment, because Emma knew Lord Royden only had eyes for his wife.

Once Sarah left, Emma composed a short note to the vicar's wife asking if her son could spend a week with them a week hence. Having had Abel over at the manor many nights, she was fairly certain of acceptance, but would wait until she heard back before mentioning it to Jamie.

Then she went upstairs to look through her wardrobe for something suitable for a week-long house party. It wasn't that she didn't have suitable clothing, she just didn't like bringing attention to herself. As a widow of modest means, she deliberately kept to herself. If it wasn't for Jamie, she'd have declined all attempts to befriend her and kept completely out of sight.

She fingered an emerald silk ballgown. Sarah had given it to her last year when she was increasing and couldn't wear it herself. Emma had planned to wear it to the annual Twelfth Night ball at Calderbrooke, but Jamie had come down with a putrid throat, so she'd remained home with him that night. Would there be an opportunity this week? Did she dare wear it?

Emma wasn't vain, but she knew the jewel-toned gown would be stunning with her white skin and red-gold hair. She was still young and comely, and a number of gentlemen in the immediate area had already cast their gazes in her direction. Fortunately, she was not available—even if she wanted to be. Which she didn't.

She was not a widow.

And she had no wish to be subject to a man again.

The last one had broken her heart.

She closed the doors on her thoughts and turned away from the wardrobe. She'd just tell Mary to pack something suitable for a week's stay at Calderbrooke and leave it at that.

The slamming of a door and running feet had her smiling, even before she heard the boyish voice.

"Mama?"

Hurrying into the hall, she called, "Up here, Jamie."

He met her on the stairs, his face ruddy from the raw wind outside, his auburn hair windblown and wild. For the past few days, he'd been hoping for snow, but so far none had fallen. She was glad of the reprieve, for once it began to snow they were housebound. Jamie might love the snow, but he didn't handle the cold well, so she was vigilant about how long he could stay outside.

"I was at Abel's when your note came," he said without preamble. "Mrs. Wight said I was welcome to stay for as long as I wished, and she told me to tell you so."

She laughed at his boyish enthusiasm. "And how long do you wish to stay?"

"A week will be long enough," he replied in all seriousness. "I like Abel, but his brothers are pests sometimes."

"Then perhaps it's fortunate you do not have any siblings of your own."

He wrinkled his nose at her, and she smiled down at him. Despite his antipathy toward Abel's siblings, he'd told her more than once that he wished he had a brother or sister to play with. Especially on those days when they were housebound because of the weather.

She wanted to tell him the truth—he had a sister. But she couldn't bear all the questions that would bring. Or the memories that would surface with them. No, he was better off not knowing she'd deprived him of a family in order to save herself.

"You must be losing your touch, Lion, old boy," Viscount Royden observed as he watched his opponent's ball spin neatly out of the pocket of the billiard table. "Scotland's made you soft."

The amused chuckle that came from Viscount Lanyon was genuine as he observed his friend taking his place. "Not any more so than you, I suspect," came the reply.

Royden took his shot and neatly pocketed two balls. He looked up at his friend and grinned.

"Been practicing, have we?" taunted Lion.

"Obviously more than you have," came the reply. "What have you been doing up there?"

Lion laughed. "Obviously not whiling my time away playing billiards. Been bored for the last nine months have we, Max?"

"Bored? Me?" Royden tried to sound offended. "You haven't spent much time in my wife's company, so I will allow the comment to pass."

The familiar bantering with a good friend was just what Lion needed these days. He watched Royden cross the carpet and refill his glass from the sideboard. What would his friend think if he knew what Lion had actually been doing up north?

Lion took a hearty swig of the amber liquid, feeling it burn all the way down to his stomach. Turning, he paced across the carpet to the window and stared out at the stark November landscape. The weak sun cast its rays through tree branches bereft of leaves. By northern England and Scotland standards, it was only nippy, but here it was cold indeed. Winter was not far off. At nearly four in the afternoon, the sun was setting fast.

"Your Sarah is a beauty, I'll grant you." *She wouldn't hold a candle to my Emma.* "One wonders what she saw in you."

Max laughed. "It was a near thing."

Two women walked by, both swathed from head to toe in fashionable woolen cloaks, fur muffs, scarves and bonnets. Although he hadn't been formally introduced to her yet, having arrived while she was out, he recognized Lady Royden when she turned and glanced toward the house. The other woman did not look, but he noted a lock of what looked to be red hair had escaped her bonnet and trailed over a slim shoulder. His interest was piqued and he willed her to turn as well, but she didn't. Moments later the two women turned a corner and were lost from view.

The door to the billiard room opened and he turned to see

Max's father, the Earl of Calderbrooke, enter with another white-haired gentleman. Viscount Lakersby, if he remembered correctly, Max's father-in-law.

"Ahh, so this is where you've been hiding," the earl teased.

"Hiding?" Max responded. "I hardly think playing a game of billiards qualifies as hiding."

"That's what Sarah would call it," Lakersby added.

"Especially since we have guests," the earl finished.

"You do realize, Father, that all those guests are friends of yours, not mine or Sarah's?" Max crossed to the sideboard again. "Brandy or whiskey?" he asked the two fathers.

They both opted for brandy and he poured generously for both.

Lion remained by the window as the other three took seats by the fire, the earlier billiard game forgotten. Listening to the three of them debate the merits of who had been invited to witness the christening of the newest addition to the Calderbrooke line made him smile. He was reminded that barely a year and a half ago, he'd returned home from London after investigating Max's brother's activities and searching for information of his own. He'd been able to help Max, but his own search had turned up empty.

Suddenly feeling as if the walls were closing in on him, he downed the last of his drink and turned to the trio.

"If you'll excuse me, I think I'll go for a walk before it gets dark."

Donning his coat and gloves, he set out toward the lake. It was a short walk, and not far from the house, giving him time to think.

Max hadn't asked, but he knew eventually the question would come up. Why hadn't he brought his wife with him? Last year, when they met in Scotland, it had been easy to tell Max his wife was living with his parents at Edenvale. He had no idea what he'd say this year.

The wind had calmed, but the air was cold, the sky clear, its fading reds and golds reflected in the smooth surface of the lake. He closed his eyes, and the fiery sunset colors coalesced into a riot of curls around a smooth oval face with eyes the color of jade.

Emma.

Filling his lungs with the cool air, he gave himself up to the memories.

She had been little more than a waif the first time he'd seen her. A four-year-old orphan brought home by his parents after a visit to relatives in Edinburgh. It hadn't taken her long to settle in, to become the daughter his mother had desperately wished for. And it hadn't taken much longer for the two of them to become inseparable.

His older brother hadn't paid her much attention, disdaining her as a worthless girl. Charles had been too busy following in their father's footsteps.

Life changed when he went off to school. He and Emma lost some of the closeness they'd once shared—and she grew up. He still remembered the shock of seeing her at fifteen. She had blossomed, developing the body of a woman with curves in all the right places, petal-soft skin, and a mane of fiery silk that reached to her waist. At twenty, he fell instantly in lust.

He might have been able to control his impulses if she hadn't come to his room one night, shaking and in tears, after having fought off Charles's drunken advances.

Opening his eyes, he turned to look at Calderbrooke. He and Max had met when they purchased commissions. They were assigned to the same regiment and quickly became friends. Both being second sons had provided more common ground, although he'd often thought the minute's difference in Max's situation was worse than the four years' difference between he and his brother.

After Waterloo, he'd accompanied Max home before heading back to Edenvale in early August, only to learn Emma had disappeared. Her desertion might not have been so shocking except for what she'd chosen to take with her and what she'd chosen to leave behind. When his brother died two years later and he became Viscount Lanyon, he'd intensified his search to no avail.

With the sun gone, the chill in the air was more pronounced. Shaking off the depressing memories, he headed back inside. It was near tea time, and everyone would be gathering in the drawing room. Arriving two days late, he was the only one not acquainted with the rest of the guests, and he knew his host expected to remedy that as soon as possible.

Max was crossing the foyer as Lion emerged from the rear hallway. Stopping only long enough to give the butler his coat and gloves, he joined Max at the door to the drawing room.

"You're just in time," Max said. "Sarah wanted you to meet Mrs. Laughlin. She's to be David's godmother. I think the Bishop will want to speak to you both before the ceremony tomorrow."

Chapter Two

Emma was bored. Seated in a wing chair near the fireplace, she was only marginally aware of the chattering going on around her. Lady Marleton and her daughter, Annalise, sat on a sofa nearby, but those two ladies weren't interested in including her in their conversation once they discovered she knew no one in London. She didn't mind. They only seemed interested in the most salacious gossip about people she'd never heard of. She was glad not to have to socialize with them on a regular basis. How did Sarah put up with such empty-headedness?

Setting her cup and saucer on the table beside her chair, she soaked up the warmth of the fire and shut out Annalise's high-pitched giggle. It wasn't often she had time on her hands. The last two days had been relaxing and restful. Although she did miss Jamie. He, on the other hand, was likely having too much fun to have missed her much.

"Who's that?" Annalise's breathless question caught Emma's attention.

"I don't know," was the reply. "But perhaps we should find out." Lady Marleton made to rise, but Annalise grabbed her arm.

"He's coming this way. Maybe Lord Royden will introduce us."

Emma's chair faced the two women, who faced the door.

Unable to satisfy her own curiosity without bringing attention to herself, she watched the younger woman sit up straighter and paste a bright smile on her face. *Heaven help whoever it is.* She could only hope the man, for that's surely who had captured the young woman's attention, was already married or otherwise taken.

"Ahh, here she is," she heard Lord Royden say. "Mrs. Laughlin, I'd like to introduce you to someone."

Wonderful, she thought as the two women looked daggers at her. Rising from her chair, she glanced at Sarah's husband then at the man beside him.

There was a sudden roaring in her ears as she looked up at the one person she never thought she'd see again. Her heart rate doubled, and she grabbed the back of the chair to keep herself upright. Through a fog, she heard Lord Royden make the introductions.

"Mrs. Laughlin, Viscount Lanyon. He is to be David's godfather, so Sarah insisted I introduce you."

Emma could not make herself move. She was aware Lord Lanyon watched her curiously, yet she instinctively knew he was as surprised as she. Her first reaction was to turn tail and run, but a quick scan of the room reminded her where she was and she squelched the impulse. She took a deep breath. Calm. She needed to calm down.

Lanyon bowed. "A pleasure, Mrs. Laughlin." Did she imagine the slight hesitation before her name?

An automatic curtsy on wobbly legs saved her from having to speak, but not long enough for her choosing. About to stammer out something, she was saved when Lady Marleton unknowingly came to her rescue.

"You must have just arrived, my lord," she interrupted. Emma knew by the stiffening of Lanyon's shoulders that he did not want to turn and acknowledge the woman, but manners won out.

As stormy gray eyes slid away from hers, so did the paralysis that had stricken her. Busy gathering her skirts, she did not pay attention to the exchange between them, nor did she realize he'd turned back to her just as she was about to escape, until she looked up again. Lord Royden's puzzled expression told her all she needed to know about her strange behavior, but she was too aware of the dismay growing inside, and that time had just run out on her freedom.

Sarah joined the small group and addressed her husband. "I see you finally found her."

He responded with a smile. "Yes. But perhaps we should adjourn to the library to discuss tomorrow's grand event."

There was nothing to discuss. They all knew that. Sarah glanced from her husband, to her, to Lanyon, and came to her own conclusions. "A great idea." She stepped between them and linked arms with Emma, drawing her away.

The cool air of the foyer dumped Emma out of her trance, and she stopped abruptly.

"Is there something wrong, Emma?" Sarah's concerned voice told her she'd noticed Emma's unusual behavior. "You're looking a little pale."

She took a deep breath and tried to still her trembling limbs.

"I'm just a bit tired. Nothing serious. I think I just need a short rest." She turned to Sarah. "I'm not used to being around so many people. It wears on me."

Sarah laughed. "Then 'tis good you have no need for a Season. The incessant partying is fun in the beginning, but I vow by the end of it, you are glad to be headed to the country."

Footsteps echoed down the hall and panic engulfed her. "Please excuse me, Sarah. I will speak to you later." Then she turned and fled up the stairs.

In the pretty blue-and-white bedroom she'd been given, she locked the door then collapsed into a chair before the fire. Once the shaking began she could not stop, and the more she tried, the worse it became. Closing her eyes did nothing, as memories rushed at her, breaking down the wall she'd erected around them, overwhelming her to the point of nausea.

"Whore!"

The voice lashed her and she flinched. Even after five years, the memory still had the ability to cause her physical pain. As the past rose up to taunt her, pain sliced through her soul, and she gasped for air as she squeezed her eyes shut. But the tears would not be held back, a deluge she was unable to contain as she relived that April day. The day she'd last seen a pair of cold, gray eyes and the look of shock, disgust and revulsion that accompanied the accusation.

Had she known that he knew Max? The name hadn't jogged any memory when she first met Sarah, or even before when she'd met Max's twin brother. Calderbrooke had meant nothing to her when she'd first arrived, beyond learning it was the principal seat of an earl of the same name. She'd been so relieved to have a place of her own. A place to raise her son independently, but still within the protection of her family. She hadn't looked any farther.

Lion watched Sarah and Emma go. He and Royden followed them moments later, but not fast enough. Sarah was standing in the foyer when the two men appeared. There was a concerned expression on her face as she looked up the stairs.

Emma was nowhere to be seen.

"What happened?" Sarah turned on her husband.

"Where?" he countered.

"In the drawing room. I've never seen Emma so agitated. Not even when Jamie fell out of that tree and broke his arm was she this upset." She looked at him, wondering if he had any answers.

He did, but he wasn't certain he was willing to tell them. Yet he knew he owed them some explanation.

"Let's go into the library," Royden said, turning his wife in that direction.

Once there, Max turned to Lion. "Sarah and Emma have become fast friends," he said, "so she's a bit over-protective. But"—he turned to Sarah—"blaming Lion is going a bit far."

"Lion?"

He smiled. "Short for Lionel, my lady. You may call me Lion or Lanyon."

"I see." She studied him through pale blue eyes brimming with curiosity. "Then you may call me Sarah." The grouping of three chairs the men had occupied earlier still sat near the fire. Sarah took one then looked up at him. "So, what did you do to terrify Emma?"

Max snorted. "He did nothing. I merely introduced them."

Lion noted the skepticism that crossed her face. He didn't blame her. Emma had said nothing at all, only stared at him through large green eyes in a face devoid of color. She'd managed a curtsy and, if it wasn't for that busybody, Lady Marleton, might have responded. Her reaction left no doubt she'd been shocked at seeing him.

"I'm afraid 'tis true, my lady," he said now, "however, I suspect Emma reacted the way she did because I was the last person she expected to see. The surprise, by the way, was mutual."

"So, you know Emma?" she asked.

His attempt at a smile probably looked more like a grimace. He did and he didn't. "I have been searching for her for nearly five years," he explained instead. It was obvious he was in for a thinly veiled interrogation.

"Why?"

He glanced over at Max, who had taken the last chair but not participated in the conversation, then sighed as he turned his attention back to Sarah. Why? There were so many reasons, he didn't know where to start. Perhaps he ought to just give her the most obvious one.

"Perhaps I just wanted to know where my wife and son were."

Sarah sat back in her chair and frowned at him. "Emma's a widow." He shook his head. "Then why would she say so?"

"Perhaps she thought so," Max spoke for the first time. "You were at Waterloo with me. There was so much confusion in the aftermath that many men were thought dead, but turned up alive, sometimes months later."

He did not contradict Max's plausible explanation, but Sarah wasn't convinced.

"I thought your family name was Cantrell. Yet her name is Laughlin."

He had no answer to that. Laughlin wasn't even Emma's maiden name. He had no idea where she'd gotten it.

"I have no explanation for that."

Sarah's eyes narrowed. "Perhaps she didn't want to be found."

Lady Royden was too shrewd, he realized, but there were

some things she would not learn from him.

She had pulled herself together, but nothing could disguise her red-rimmed eyes. Emma sat before the dressing table's glass and examined her face for other telltale signs of the emotional upheaval of the last two hours. The smile she tried was strained, and didn't reach her eyes. She conjured up a picture of Jamie, and the smile warmed a bit.

Sighing, she rose from the padded seat. At least she looked presentable. The russet velvet gown showed her to advantage, although the green would have been better. She'd planned to wear that tomorrow per Sarah's request. She didn't want to embarrass her hostess in front of her stylish guests by looking like a country mouse.

The clock on the fireplace chimed the hour of seven. Time to go.

Ignoring the fluttering in her stomach, she took a deep breath and headed for the door. The stern talking-to she'd given herself ran through her head. She would not allow Lion's appearance to shake her again. Her earlier discomfort had been due to surprise. Now that she knew he was here, she could steel herself against him.

Going back over the scene in the drawing room, she remembered Max introducing him as Viscount Lanyon. There was only one reason why Lion would be using that title.

Was it wrong to be pleased over someone's death? Perhaps tomorrow at the church, she might say a prayer for Charles's immortal soul, but today she felt nothing but relief. She could return without fear if she wanted to, but it still did not solve the problem of what to do about Lion.

At least one thing turned out to be right, and a small smile of satisfaction crept across her face. He *was* taken. That ought to keep Lady Marleton from throwing Annalise at him. Unless he was holding himself out as single too.

Lord Owllerton met her at the door. He was one of the younger men who had arrived escorting a parent. The heir to a marquess, he reminded her a bit of an owl when he used his monocle to survey those around him. She suspected the monocle was for more than just show when he used it to carefully pour her a glass of sherry.

"Are you enjoying yourself, Mrs. Laughlin?"

The polite conversation opener was delivered with an air of ennui one so young should not possess.

"I am, thank you. And you?" She was just as bad, considering she didn't particularly want an answer.

"I find I am, although I did not expect to do so when Mama insisted I accompany her."

"Do you plan to escape when your father arrives, then?"

He leaned closer to her, speaking in a low voice. "Not if you do not wish me to."

She nearly choked on her drink at the intimate tone, and stepped back quickly. "I am neutral on the subject, my lord," she said primly.

His warm gaze rested on her bare neckline, and she felt the slow flush that was fast becoming angry indignation. She was about to turn and walk away when she spied Lion across the room watching her. Cursing herself for letting his presence dictate her actions, she smiled up at the young earl while putting him in his place.

"If you are looking for a dalliance, I suggest you look elsewhere. I am not available."

Unabashed, he responded with a smile of his own. "My

27

loss."

He took her at her word, however, and dinner passed without incident. The young earl had been assigned to take her in to dinner and proved to be an amusing companion. She was thankful for his attention as he mostly kept her mind off Lion, who was seated further along the table beside Annalise.

She could feel his intent regard, and it did nothing for her peace of mind. More than once, she had to restrain herself from looking in his direction. By the time the ladies retired to the drawing room, she felt drained. She might have taken her usual seat near the fire, but she wanted to be able to see the door this time and so opted for a window seat. When Sarah joined her, she prepared herself to satisfy her friend's curiosity.

"I won't ask," Sarah began, "but I hope you know you can talk to me if you need to."

Emma hadn't expected such understanding. She knew she owed Sarah some explanation, if only to put her mind at ease regarding the person she'd chosen as her son's godmother.

"It is rather a long story," she said slowly, "but I do want you to know, I never thought Lion would ever find me."

Sarah smiled. "Unfortunately, he would have eventually because he and Max are close friends. I suppose if you'd known, you would never have come to this area."

"True. But I'm glad I did, even though now I have to decide what to do."

"He told us you're married, and implied that Jamie is his son."

She nodded. "It's true, but I had no idea he was a viscount. His older brother must have passed away."

"Does that make a difference now?"

"Only to Jamie," she replied as the men began to trickle

into the room.

Lion was talking to the earl as he entered. She took the opportunity to study him while he was engaged. He'd changed from the young man she once knew. The Lion she'd fallen in love with had been little more than a boy. At twenty, he had been too young to be saddled with the responsibility of a wife and child, but there had been no other option.

The person she'd been introduced to earlier was a man. Tall and commanding, he dwarfed nearly every other male in the room. Broad shoulders filled out his black evening coat, tapering down to slim hips and long, muscular legs. His brown hair gleamed in the candlelight, brushed back from a high, intelligent forehead above eyes the color of polished pewter.

"Would you prefer not to be left alone with him?"

The question from Sarah caught her off guard. She wasn't afraid of him. He'd never physically hurt her, but she wasn't sure what he thought of her. And she didn't dare ask.

"I-I don't know," she responded truthfully. "I don't suppose I can avoid him completely since I promised to stay the entire week."

Sarah's sympathy gave her a measure of security. "I wouldn't hold it against you if you left tomorrow, after the ceremony."

"I know, but it wouldn't accomplish anything. Even if you refused to tell him, he would discover my whereabouts."

Running away would gain her nothing. She knew eventually she'd have to face him. And there was Jamie to consider.

Dinner had been excruciating.

Did Max's wife have a mean streak? Or maybe it was a protective streak. Either way, seating him beside Lord Marleton's daughter had to have been punishment for frightening Emma. He hadn't felt any guilt at all informing the little she-cat of his marital status. He wished he'd been able to tell her that the woman she'd made such derisive remarks about was his wife, but for now, he chose to keep Emma's secrets. Whatever might happen in the days to come, he did not want to embarrass her in front of people who would have no qualms about shredding her character.

The young pup assigned to escort Emma in to dinner had come close to being strangled with his own monocle ribbon more than once, although Emma didn't seem to mind his obvious ogling.

Max interrupted his dour thoughts. "Do you want me to remove my wife from her position?"

Lion glanced over to where Sarah and Emma sat close together in conversation. Did he want to try to force her to talk to him now? Could he? Six years ago, he might have been able to, but he didn't know her now. She'd been on her own for the last five years. How much had she changed?

He shook his head. "No. I've caused enough disruption for one day. Maybe tomorrow."

Max looked at him for a very long moment, then shrugged and said, "She can't go far, so tomorrow might be better after all."

"Can't go far?"

"I meant she doesn't live very far from here. In fact, I wouldn't be surprised to see Jamie at the christening tomorrow. He's staying with the vicar and his family while she's here."

"So they live close?"

"McKeown Manor. A small property on the southern edge of

Calderbrooke. I think she told Sarah it belongs to her brother."

This was news to Lion. Especially since her brother, Lord Englevyn, told him he had no idea where she was. Brother and sister had obviously conspired to keep her location a secret. It was a grim realization for him that, as Sarah remarked earlier, she obviously had not wanted to be found.

Lord Owllerton approached her again and Lion's gut seized at the warm smile she bestowed upon him. Were they lovers? Were there others in the room who had sampled her favors? His jaw clenched at the thought and he turned away.

He thought he needed a drink. Once in possession of the glass of amber liquid however, he discovered his taste had soured and put it down on a table. Disgusted with himself, he walked out of the room. Watching Emma was making him insane.

In the library, he settled himself in a chair near the fire to think. He'd almost given up ever finding her. Now he had, he had no idea what to do. In the past, whenever he imagined finding her, she had always been contrite for leaving and happy to return with him to Edenvale. It never occurred to him she would be living as a widow, denying his very existence.

And Jamie. What had she told their son?

She was pleased for Sarah, and she wouldn't let anything interfere with her happiness. So Emma told herself as she sat across from Max and Sarah in the coach headed for the village church. It would be an easier promise to keep without the presence of the man sitting next to her. The low-hanging clouds of a week ago were gone, and the sun shone brilliantly in a cloudless sky. The chill November air was crisp but the occupants of the conveyance were warm, especially young

Master David Maxwell Stephen Jesse Dayton who resembled a sausage, bundled as he was in a number of layers and asleep in his mother's arms.

"Nurse says he's a very good baby," Sarah was saying. "I don't suspect she will still think that when he is two."

Max chuckled. "By the time he's four, she'll be cursing his very existence."

"I suspect he will be into everything by then," she agreed.

"Emma certainly was," Lion commented.

Stunned, she turned to look at him as Sarah asked, "And how would you know?"

"Because that's when she came to live with us."

Sarah turned pale blue eyes on her. "You two grew up together?"

Emma could only nod, her voice having deserted her completely.

"Her parents, two sisters and a brother all died from scarlet fever," Lion explained. "She was the only one who survived—and an older brother who was at school at the time. Her mother and mine were distant cousins."

The coach came to a stop, relieving her of the obligation to join the conversation. Lion handed her down, and she wished she could have ignored the spark that traveled up her arm at his touch. For a moment, she was fifteen again and watching him arrive home from London.

She'd been gazing out of a second floor window as he rode up the drive, his dark brown hair glinting in the sun. Controlling his powerful stallion easily, he sat tall and regal in the saddle. Forcing herself to calm down, she came down the stairs as he was entering the foyer. When he looked up and their eyes met, she fell hopelessly in love.

Pushing the memories away, she turned and glanced around the crowd. She couldn't decide whether she hoped Jamie was there or he'd managed to stay away. Lion offered her his arm, knowing she couldn't refuse without someone noticing. Feeling his solidly muscled forearm through the sleeve of his coat only made her more aware of him and reminded her of her observations of the evening before. Once inside the small church, she was grateful for the opportunity to step away from him when Sarah handed her the baby.

It was all over thirty minutes later. Young David slept through the entire service.

As they emerged from the church, most of the crowd was dispersing. Standing silently beside Lion, she looked over at Sarah and Max. She'd never envied her friend before, but now with Lion standing beside her, she wished he would look at her the way Max looked down at Sarah. So much would change.

"Mama!" Jamie materialized at her side. She felt Lion stiffen as she turned to respond.

Smiling down at him, she said, "I was wondering if you were here."

"I only just came," he replied, "but you'll never guess what?"

She laughed down at him. "If I'll never guess, then you'd best just tell me."

"I taught Bobo to jump over a log and he did it twice!"

She frowned. Bobo was Jamie's pony. Her brother, Thomas, had given it to him for his fifth birthday.

"That is splendid, darling, but I thought we agreed you wouldn't try to teach Bobo any tricks unless Sam was with you."

She hated to watch the excitement fade from his eyes. Eyes

the same color as his father's.

"But he wasn't hurt."

"I'm glad of it, but you remember what Sam said about ponies."

He nodded solemnly. "That if you teach them something wrong, it will be hard to teach them the same thing the proper way."

She reached down and hugged him. "I'll bet if you showed Sam what you taught Bobo, he'll help you make sure it's right."

"You think so?" His enthusiasm returned.

"I would guess so," she confirmed. "But no more tricks until we get home. All right?"

He returned her hug. "All right." Then he turned and ran off, joining another boy a short distance away.

She was aware of Lion still standing beside her and that he'd witnessed the entire exchange. He didn't wait until she turned back.

"Bobo, I take it, is a pony?"

She looked up and was taken aback by the expression of disapproval on his face. "Yes," she answered. "Thomas sent it to him for his fifth birthday."

"And Sam?"

"One of the stablehands. He's been teaching Jamie about horses."

"I see." The response was little more than a growl. Now what? Jamie hadn't harmed the pony, she was certain. And Sam would make sure Bobo was fine before allowing Jamie to teach him any more tricks.

The ride back to Calderbrooke was accomplished mostly in silence, except for the occasional fussing of the infant as he awakened. Emma reached over and smoothed her fingers over the downy skin. It had been a long time since she played with an infant. Longing rose up in her, but she pushed it back. It was unlikely she'd ever have another child. Yearning for one was useless.

Lion held her back when she would have followed Max and Sarah up the front steps of Calderbrooke.

"Walk with me."

She bristled at the command, instantly defensive. "No."

His hand tightened on her elbow. "We can either speak outside where there is little likelihood of being overheard, or inside where the rest of Max and Sarah's guests might decide to eavesdrop. Your choice."

Pressing her lips together, she conceded the point to him.

"Very well," she said, "but make it short." Then she turned and stalked off. Moments later he was striding beside her, easily keeping up with her furious walking pace.

They strolled in silence, circling the house until they neared the lake. "Are we headed anywhere in particular?" he asked in a conversational tone.

She stopped and looked around her. "I suppose this is far enough from the house." She didn't want to get too close. It would be too easy to be taken in by him again. He reached out to touch her, but she stepped out of his reach, crossing her arms over her chest. He dropped his hand to his side with a sigh.

"I won't hurt you, Emma."

She didn't respond. It would do no good to tell him he'd done so before. "What did you want to speak about?"

"You, and Jamie." When she continued to look up at him, he thrust his hand through his hair in frustration. "I want you to return to Edenvale with me."

"No." She had to force the word over the lump in her throat.

"Why not?"

"There is nothing there for me any longer." And it held too many painful memories. "I have made a home for us here."

"You realize that Jamie is my heir and, as such, should grow up at Edenvale."

"I suppose you feel that gives you all the cards."

"Don't make this a war, Emma. I don't want to be at war with you. I just want my wife and son back."

She turned away, looking out over the glassy surface of the lake. It was so still, it looked like polished glass and sturdy enough to walk on. But, like Lion's words, there were hidden currents and danger beneath the beauty presented to the world.

"It's too late for that," she responded in a near whisper he had to bend to hear.

"Why?"

She closed her eyes on the peaceful sight before her, and his face appeared. The gray eyes raked over her in disgust, his contempt a tangible thing. She wrapped her arms around herself to keep the trembling at bay and calm her churning stomach.

"Because it is," was the only thing she could say. Then she hurried away. Away from the hateful memories. Away from the pain of his presence. Away from the destruction of her dreams.

Chapter Three

Lion watched her walk away and sighed in frustration. He'd never make headway if she kept running. Perhaps it was time to change tactics. Talking wasn't working.

He had to admit, though, she'd matured into a beautiful woman. A woman who, under other circumstances, he might have done everything he could to get her into his bed. Right now, however, he'd have to do everything he could just to keep her from running away.

The afternoon was cooling rapidly, and his breath misted before his face. It would be simpler if he could just seduce her, but she obviously wouldn't let him close enough. So now what? Could he get to her through Jamie? Probably. But he didn't want to use his son that way.

Thinking about Jamie brought a fresh surge of anger. For five years she'd deprived him of his son. He'd missed giving Jamie his first pony and teaching him to ride. Holidays and birthdays too. Yet, he also felt some pride in the sturdy little boy he didn't know. A circumstance he would remedy as soon as he could. Regardless of what she might have told the boy, he fully intended Jamie to know who he was.

She couldn't avoid him forever. He had time on his side. Now that he'd found her, she would not disappear on him again.

Following at a slower pace, he wondered if he could impose on Max for a little longer. It would be nice to spend some time catching up with his friend, but perhaps Max might also be able to help him with Emma. It occurred to him Max might know more about his wife and son than he did. Perhaps a longer conversation was in order.

He didn't expect to find Emma in the drawing room with the rest of the guests preparing for tea. Most of the men were probably in the billiard room, but he noticed Lord Owllerton among the few who hadn't completely deserted. The young lordling's presence wouldn't have bothered him if he hadn't been sitting near Emma, speaking to her in what looked to be a far too intimate manner.

Max was talking to the bishop. He remembered Max telling him the elderly man was a distant cousin. Max and Sarah would have been content to have the local vicar, whose living Calderbrooke provided, christen their son, but his father insisted the bishop would feel slighted if he wasn't asked to officiate.

Lion was about to leave to join any of the men who might be in the billiard room when he noticed Lord Owllerton leave Emma's side. Not one to waste an opening, he moved swiftly across the room before she noticed his presence. Sarah was handing her a cup when he reached her. Emma said nothing as he took the recently vacated place beside her, but he felt her stiffen.

He didn't understand why he seemed to make her so uncomfortable. It wasn't as if he'd ever hurt or abused her. She should know she had nothing to fear from him. But perhaps that was one of the puzzles he needed to figure out. For now, however, he would try to keep to less personal topics.

Sarah noticed him and asked if he wanted tea or something

stronger. He opted for tea. Once settled with his cup, he turned to Emma.

"Tell me about Jamie."

Surprised, she looked over at him. "What do you want to know?"

"Whatever you want to tell me," he replied. "Is he normally in good health? Wild, or prone to tantrums? Spoiled?"

She laughed and he nearly dropped his cup at the unexpected sight. With eyes alight, her face alive with amusement, she was stunning. He had forgotten, he realized, what had initially drawn him to her.

"Of course he's spoiled," she told him. "But he's not selfish or vain, if that's what you mean. He's in reasonably good health, but he doesn't handle the cold well. He tends to love the snow, but he catches chills much too easily for my taste. As for being wild—he's a boy. I suppose he gets into the normal things boys get into. Lord Royden has taken him fishing and riding occasionally. And I think Calderbrooke's gamekeeper taught him to snare rabbits earlier this year."

Lion was amazed. Not at all that she imparted, but that she talked freely to him. Gone was the Emma who shunned his presence and refused to answer his questions. The woman in her place was beautiful, warm and outgoing.

"Does he have a tutor?"

She shook her head. "The vicar has tutored him along with his own sons. He reads, writes and is learning Greek and Latin. I tried to interest him in learning the pianoforte, but he refuses to apply himself. Although he doesn't mind listening to me play."

The key, Lion realized, was getting her to talk about Jamie. As a mother, Jamie was her pride and joy. And as he listened to her talk and asked her questions about their son, he was astonished more than once at what she revealed. At the same time, he experienced an unfamiliar emotion as he watched the expressions move across her face.

It took him a few moments to realize he was jealous. Jealous of the bond between mother and son and the shared experiences he'd missed. Jealous of the time she'd deprived him of—time that could not be reclaimed.

By the time the women began drifting off to begin preparing for the evening, he and Emma had shared an enjoyable conversation, and he found himself intrigued. Much of what he thought he knew about her conflicted with the impression he'd gained from their chat.

As he went upstairs to dress for dinner, he went back over his encounters with Emma. Each one provided him with pieces of a puzzle that was by no means complete. Would the completed puzzle provide him with all the answers he needed?

Emma found it amusing Sarah refused to call the assembly that evening a ball, despite it being held in the grandly opulent Calderbrooke ballroom. Hundreds of candles shone from three massive chandeliers, reflected in the mirrored panels scattered throughout the room. The walls that weren't mirrored were covered with cream-on-cream striped silk, trimmed with oak framing which matched the highly polished floor.

"It's lovely," Emma said.

"As are you," Sarah responded. "I was right about how well that gown would become you."

Emma looked down at the emerald ball gown. It was quite the loveliest thing she'd ever owned and she knew, without being vain, she looked her best in it. As she and Sarah stood together at the top of the stairs, she reminded herself that this was her very first ball, regardless of what Sarah wanted to call it.

At eighteen, not only had she already been married, but a mother as well. A season at that time would have been bittersweet, especially with Lion away. If she had known of the disaster to befall her the next year, she would have jumped at the chance anyway. She suppressed a sigh. No use wishing the past was different. It was gone and nothing could change it. For now, she only hoped to remember enough of those long ago dancing lessons not to embarrass herself.

Lord Owllerton met her at the bottom of the stairs and requested the next set. It was a quadrille, and she was proud of herself at its conclusion. She only missed a step once, when she came face-to-face with Lion as part of the pattern.

"Lord Owllerton is very attentive," Sarah remarked at one point.

Emma smiled. "Yes, he is. And he has been a perfect gentleman after the first evening he was my dinner partner."

"Let's hope he continues to be," Sarah remarked cryptically. "He doesn't have the best of reputations, but I've always considered him harmless."

A country dance had just concluded when Max and Lion approached them.

"I have requested a waltz as the next dance," Max declared, holding his hand out to Sarah.

She batted her eyelashes playfully at him. "Hmmm. I don't know if I should engage in such a scandalous dance with you."

Max merely grinned at her and replied, "No matter. I'll dance with this divine creature standing next to you, then."

Emma laughed at him. "I'm afraid I value Sarah's friendship too much, my lord. Perhaps someone else would oblige." Max gave her a mournful look that reminded her too much of Jamie when he wanted something he couldn't have. "Goodness, Sarah, how do you manage him?"

"Besides, she's taken," Lion interjected.

A familiar thrill shot through her at Lion's words, and she had to ruthlessly crush the urge to move closer to him. Instead, she turned to give him a scathing setdown. ·

The orchestra struck up the next song at that moment and, without waiting for her to agree, Lion swept her into his arms and out onto the floor. Too busy keeping track of the steps, she was unable to speak for the first few minutes.

"I had forgotten how lovely you are, Emma."

Her head snapped up and she stumbled. Lion steadied her without missing a step.

"Careful," he murmured. "Now is not the time to cause a scene. You don't want to ruin Sarah's night, do you?"

His hand burned her through the layers of silk and cotton. A slow flush heated her cheeks, and she dropped her gaze to his cravat. It was easier to concentrate that way rather than looking into his face. The gentle strength in his arms kept her upright while butterflies took up residence in her stomach. She refused to acknowledge how easy it would be to melt into him and let bygones be bygones. It wouldn't last anyway. Eventually the aversion would return and, if she wasn't careful, she would be the one left with a scarred and broken heart—again.

For tonight, however, she could close her eyes and imagine Lion was still hers. That he didn't despise her for the past. That he loved her as he once had, and wanted her to return because he wanted her, not merely because their son was his heir.

She took a deep breath as he spun her through a turn, inhaling his scent and feeling it seep into her blood. The combination of sandalwood and something that was uniquely

Lion transported her into the past. Back before her disgrace. Before Lion looked at her with a mixture of disbelief and disgust.

Blinking back the tears that threatened, she once again envisioned her son's face, alight with joy, to regain her composure. Tonight she would throw caution to the wind and enjoy herself. She would pretend Lion was a handsome stranger and allow herself to bask in his company.

The decision made, she steeled herself to look up into his face and smiled.

"I would never do anything to hurt Sarah. She has been a wonderful friend to me," she told him.

"I'm glad to hear that. Max has been inviting me to visit for the past year, but I have always declined because I was busy with other obligations. More than once, I nearly came, but something always seemed to come up."

What would she have done had he arrived last year, or even earlier this year? Would she have uprooted Jamie and left again? When he was three, the only person he missed was his nurse, Mousey, but now he had friends in the village, and taking him away would mean leaving them behind.

"I should have come anyway." The eyes resting on her were warm, but a hint of suspicion lurked in the depths.

She looked away. It wouldn't do for him to see how much she wished he hadn't accepted the invitation to be David's godfather. Their meeting might have been postponed for a few more months.

He asked her a question about Jamie, and she responded with a smile. Thankful for the distraction from her disturbing thoughts, she and Lion finished the set in companionable conversation.

As he escorted her from the floor, they were met by Squire

Findley, her partner for the next set. She pushed away the disappointment at leaving Lion and allowed the squire to lead her out for a country dance.

The rest of the evening passed in a blur of partners. Lord Owllerton seemed to have appointed himself her guardian, for he managed to keep to her side when she wasn't dancing or conversing with someone. He fetched glasses of punch for her, danced with her a second time and took her in to supper. She enjoyed his company once he no longer seemed inclined to get too close.

Near the end of the evening, however, she began to have misgivings about his proprietorial air. Perhaps it had something to do with the look Lion had given her at one point, or just the feeling she had that something was not quite right. When she emerged from the retiring room after refreshing herself, Lord Owllerton was waiting for her.

"You are taking this notion of escort a bit far, my lord," she said primly.

He stopped near a curtained alcove and looked at her. "You think so?"

"Yes, in fact, I do. I am quite capable of finding my way around." Moonlight streamed through the window of the alcove, casting a pale beam onto the carpet at their feet.

"I am quite aware that you are a capable woman, madam," he replied. "And a very beautiful one at that. I only thought to shield you from all the lascivious looks you have been receiving all evening."

She arched an eyebrow. "From who else besides you?"

He chuckled. "Surely you have noticed the way Lord Lanyon looks at you?"

She felt the blush rise in her cheeks, unable to stem the telltale tide. "It means nothing," she replied.

He stepped closer. "Surely you know his reputation?"

"What reputation?"

"I've heard that before Waterloo he and Lord Royden were well known amongst the ladies. Lord Royden, of course, was not married at the time, but supposedly Lanyon was. Of course, neither he nor Royden had titles at the time, but that didn't stop them from working their way through the female ranks."

She looked away, unable to hide the sudden pain she experienced. Did it surprise her that only two months after she'd last seen him, he'd sought out other women?

Lord Owllerton reached up and turned her face back to his. His fingers were gentle on her chin, the thumb brushing over her cheek. "I didn't mean to bring you sorrow," he said softly. "I just thought you ought to know." Then he bent his head and kissed her.

Stunned, she merely stood there. It was the last thing she'd expected after he agreed to take her at her word last evening. Frozen to the spot, she vaguely felt his arm go around her back and pull her closer, but it wasn't until she heard a throat being cleared behind her that she regained her senses. Wrenching herself away from him, she turned to see Lion standing near the end of the hallway.

Mortification washed through her. What had she done? How had she let Owllerton maneuver her into such a position?

"I apologize for intruding on such an intimate moment." His eyes glittered in the muted candlelight. For a moment, she thought he would hit Owllerton. It would serve the young lord right if he did. His reaction might indicate he was jealous, but she knew he wasn't. "Sarah wondered where you'd gone."

It was a simple enough explanation, but the look in his eyes revealed his thoughts. She may as well have been caught in bed with Owllerton. The distaste she'd steeled herself against was clear in the stormy depths and she shivered. Owllerton chose that moment to step closer to her and put an arm around her shoulders. Rage surfaced in Lion's eyes and she reacted.

Shaking off the arm, she brushed past Lion without a word and hurried back to the ballroom. It would serve Owllerton right if Lion pounded him to a pulp, but she did not want to witness it. Stopping at the bottom of the stairs, she took a deep, calming breath and smoothed her features into a polite expression before seeking out Sarah.

She persevered through the rest of the evening but, despite her attempts, she never succeeded in regaining her delight in the assembly. Eventually she convinced Sarah she was tired and slipped away to her room.

Emma was partnered with another young lord for the next evening, Lord Owllerton having departed that morning. She was thankful Sarah seemed to understand she did not want to be in Lion's company as much as he seemed to want to be in hers. Despite that, she was surprised to find him waiting for her at the foot of the stairs as she descended the afternoon of her departure for home.

She was not naïve enough to think he might have left for home as she wished him to, but his first words to her as she reached the last step stopped her cold.

"I will be accompanying you home."

"Why?" The question was out before she could stop it.

"I think that should be obvious. I want to spend time with my son."

His son. Not her. Why was she disappointed? She didn't want to spend time with him. She'd spent the last day avoiding him and strengthening her defenses, so why did the fact that he wanted to accompany her home make her spirits rise?

Sarah and Max joined them. As they exited the front door, she heard Max tell Lion he was welcome to stay as long as he wished. She glanced at the shiny black equipage bearing the Edenvale crest, sitting at the foot of the stairs.

A sudden gust of wind threatened to rip her bonnet from her head, and she hugged her cloak tightly to her. The bright sunshine of two days ago had disappeared behind stormy clouds Max predicted held snow, and she sighed. She wasn't ready for winter just yet.

Lion handed her into the comfortable interior and climbed in after her. As they began to move, she started to ask if his coachman knew where they were going, but decided he'd probably received directions from the Calderbrooke coachman. They passed through the gates and turned onto the main road. She made an effort to look anywhere except at the large male seated across from her. Pretending to study the scenery was easier than actually pushing Lion's presence from her mind.

"Will Jamie already be at home when we arrive?"

Her head whipped around at the sudden question. "No. He knew I was to come home today, but he wouldn't have expected me until tea time. I suspect he will wait as long as possible before making an appearance."

"Does he enjoy being with the vicar's family that much?"

She smiled. "He enjoys playing with Abel, Reverend Wight's oldest son. He has told me before he finds Abel's brothers to be pests."

Lion's answering smile caused her heart to stutter. She turned back to the window and frowned. Why was she suddenly having these strange feelings? Like a schoolgirl in the throes of her first crush. And with Lion of all people.

The rest of the short journey was accomplished in silence. She was relieved when the coach turned into the drive. The modest Georgian manor of warm orange brick stood three stories, plus attics. The whitewashed, doric pilasters and intricate brickwork around the windows and on the chimneys lent an air of pretension to what would otherwise have been a very plain edifice. With the elaborately carved double front door, it was a picture-perfect country home.

In the four years since she'd arrived at McKeown Manor, Emma had come to love the place. When she originally asked her brother if there was anywhere on his estates she and Jamie could live undisturbed, she had not expected he would provide so handsomely for her. He had hinted it was part of the dowry Lion had every right to expect. It hadn't occurred to her she should have had a dowry. Having been raised at Edenvale, she had merely assumed she was the countess's ward. She'd determined to ask Thomas about it after she and Jamie were settled, but the years passed and she hadn't done so yet.

The low-hanging clouds seemed less threatening than when they left Calderbrooke, but that didn't stop her from casting a worried glance upward. Despite having told Lion she didn't expect him to be waiting for her, she asked after Jamie as they entered the wood-paneled foyer.

"I sent Sam for him a half hour ago, Madam," Graves replied. "With a storm blowing in, I thought to have him here before you arrived. We did not expect you back so soon."

She smiled at the butler. "I would have stayed longer, but I missed home." Jamie, on the other hand, would wait as long as he could to return. "Thank you."

Lion cleared his throat, and she turned as if remembering his presence.

"Oh, Graves, this is Lord Lanyon. He is a guest at

Calderbrooke," she said. Turning toward the drawing room, she added, "He is here to spend some time with Jamie, so when Jamie arrives would you send him to me?"

The butler accepted Lion's coat and gloves. "M'lord." Then, turning to Emma, asked, "Shall I set a third place for dinner?"

She stopped and looked back at Lion, wondering how long he intended to stay.

"Only if it will not be too much trouble," he answered the question in her eyes.

She nodded and turned to Graves, who was already responding. "No trouble at all, milord. No trouble at all. I'll just go and inform cook."

The die was cast, she thought as she entered the room overlooking the front lawns, Lion in her wake. She was thankful Lion hadn't assumed he would move in, but she had the feeling it was merely a matter of time.

She heard him close the door behind them as she stopped before one of the large windows. The wind seemed to have calmed slightly but the air was still cool. She turned and sat on the window seat so she could look out.

"Please, have a seat. I do not need you towering over me."

He chuckled as he seated himself on a sofa near the window, and the sound sent a wash of heat through her blood. Ruthlessly she pushed the feeling away.

"We should decide what to tell Jamie," she began.

"I don't think there is any question but that he should be told the truth. He's old enough—"

"No!" She gripped her hands together to keep them from shaking.

His eyes narrowed, the gray competing with the storm clouds gathering outside the window. "Why not?"

Because she didn't want him to know all the sordid details. Because she refused to let him be tainted by the details of her past. "Because...because he will ask too many questions," she stammered. "And I don't want anyone making assumptions."

"And you don't want to answer questions." He studied her for a few minutes. She stiffened her spine to keep him from seeing how nervous she really was. "So, what have you told him about me?"

"I-I...nothing. Only that you died when he was three."

"I see."

Silence fell.

"I would prefer he not know just yet. He will have to know eventually, but now is not the right time."

Lion shifted in his seat. His eyes narrowed on her before he asked, "And when do you think will be the right time to tell him you've lied to him?"

"It could have been the truth," she hedged.

"Is that what you wished for, perhaps? That I might have died on a battlefield somewhere? I'm sorry to have made this difficult for you by surviving. Perhaps you would have preferred I had not, but it's not what happened."

There was little for them to say to each other, yet she worried over what he might be thinking. Would he tell Jamie she'd lied to him? How far was he willing to go to reclaim his son? And would she be left behind once he'd done so?

"Regardless, Charles would not have married you."

Shock kept her immobilized at the possible thought that, had Lion been killed, she would have been at Charles's mercy if he found her. She was about to respond when the sound of running feet on the tiled foyer echoed loudly before the door burst open and Jamie came running across the room.

"Mama! Mama! Guess what?"

She knew he hadn't seen Lion at all when he climbed up on the seat beside her, his gray eyes alight with excitement. It was enough to banish her disturbing thoughts.

"Do I have to guess?" she asked with a smile.

"Sam said I taught Bobo just the right way. He said he would show me how to teach Bobo some new tricks too. D'you think I could show Lord Royden?"

She smiled at his infectious enthusiasm. "Maybe, but"—she took a deep breath—"perhaps you could show our new visitor first."

Jamie looked over his shoulder, noticing Lion for the first time. He scrambled off the window seat, but didn't approach him. It seemed like forever as father and son seemed to take each other's measure, and Emma's apprehension grew as the moment stretched.

"I saw you with Mama at the church," Jamie blurted. "Does that mean you're to be my new papa?"

"Jamie!" Blood rushed to her face, and she could feel the heat all the way to the roots of her hair.

He turned puzzled gray eyes on her. "That's what Abel's papa says. And that's what happened when Nan and Jeremiah went to the church together and everyone went to watch."

"I'm afraid not," Lion replied. "We only went to watch the christening of Lord and Lady Royden's new son."

"Oh." Disappointment laced that one syllable, and Emma's heart dropped. Jamie had never spoken about wanting to have a father. He had plenty of father figures around who had been willing to provide him with the activities men and boys often do together.

"Would you like to have a papa?" Lion asked.

"Yes, but I don't think Mama does." He cocked his head to the side and studied Lion for a few moments, then ventured, "Lord Royden said he could be my temporary papa until Mama brought home a new one."

Emma stared at Jamie's back in dismay. When had he said something to Lord Royden?

"I see." Lion smiled at him, and Emma felt again the warmth of his smile, even though it wasn't directed at her. "Well, Lord Royden is busy right now with his own son, so do you think I could take his place for now?"

A slow nod was Jamie's response.

"Then that's what we'll do."

"Does that mean you will be staying with us?"

Lion shook his head. "For right now, I will be staying with Lord Royden. People might begin to think bad thoughts about your mama if I stayed here, but I promise to come over every day. Do you think that will work?"

"You'll come every day?"

"If that's what you want."

"Could I tell Abel and the other boys?"

"Why would you want to do that?" she asked him. If word got around, the talk would be just as bad as if Lion had moved in.

Jamie glanced back over his shoulder at her. "Because then the other boys won't feel sorry for me because I don't have a papa."

She had nothing to say to that response, and she noticed the way Lion's mouth tightened before Jamie turned back to him. "Perhaps for a few days it will be our secret," he told Jamie. "Maybe by then your mama and I will have worked things out."

She should say something, but her mind was blank.

"In the meantime, how about if you tell me about your pony? Your mama tells me you ride quite well."

As Jamie began telling Lion about his pony, she heard the excitement return in his voice. Lion seemed to know all the right questions to ask, and she smiled to herself as he went on and on. At one point, as Jamie demonstrated how he'd taught his pony to jump a log, her eyes met Lion's over their son's head.

The delight in his eyes was unmistakable. She'd worried Jamie would bore Lion with his enthusiasm over his pony, but Lion was enjoying himself. She relaxed as relief washed over her. They might not agree on what to tell Jamie, or the rest of the area, but Jamie was important enough to put aside their differences for the moment.

She glanced out the window and noticed it had started to rain. Jamie would be disappointed, but she wasn't. The longer the snow held off, the better.

When Jamie ran out of the room in search of something to show Lion, an uncomfortable silence descended. After a few moments, Lion asked, "Did you know?"

"No." There was no use in pretending ignorance. She hadn't known Jamie was the subject of pity among the boys of the village because of an absent father.

"Would you have acted differently had you known?"

She stood and crossed the room to the bell pull. When Graves answered, she requested tea. It was a ploy to avoid Lion's question, but he refused to let the matter drop.

"Would you?" he pressed.

She faced him from across the room. "No."

He unfolded himself from the sofa and approached her.

"Why not?"

She truly had no answer he would understand, and she couldn't continue to tell him "because" when she didn't want to explain herself. He stopped before her as if waiting for an answer. Staring up at him, she was conscious of his barely contained frustration before he turned and moved away from her. Mutely she watched him prowl the room. It was too small for him, she realized, as it took only a few strides to cross from one side of the room to the other.

He stopped before the window, his broad back to the room. Was he actually examining the landscape beyond the glass or contemplating another question she would likely refuse to answer? Studying his proud carriage, she marveled again that he had once been hers. That once they had loved each other with an unquenchable passion.

A soft sigh escaped at the loss. For a short time he had been everything to her—husband, lover, protector. Then it had all gone horribly wrong. The catalyst for the disaster was gone, but she doubted anything could bridge the chasm he'd created.

The door opened and Mrs. Smythe entered, carrying the requested tea. She took her time placing the tray on the low table before the sofa, ensuring she got a good look at Lion.

"Thank you, Mrs. Smythe." The woman nodded then left as Emma took a seat before the tray. "Would you like some tea?" she asked.

She watched his shoulders rise and fall as he took a breath. When he turned to face her, she looked away from the censure in his eyes.

"If you do not help, Emma, we will never work this out."

She poured herself a cup of tea.

"There is nothing to work out. I will not return to Edenvale. There is nothing there for me except memories I would rather
54

forget." The lump of sugar she added to her tea slowly dissolved as she stirred the steaming liquid.

"And what does that mean for Jamie? Do you want me to take him from you?"

"No," she answered over the sudden lump in her throat. "But I was already preparing myself for his departure within the next year or two. Thomas said he would make arrangements for Jamie to attend school."

His face tightened. "I see."

"I suppose now you can do that if you wish. I will write to Thomas tomorrow."

Jamie burst into the room carrying a book, giving her a reprieve. The glance Lion gave her said clearly they were not finished discussing her stubbornness. For now, however, Jamie commanded his attention and, as she watched father and son interact, a reluctant sense of pride welled up within her.

Why was she such a coward? She knew she was being unreasonable. Lion had every right to wonder at her motives and reasons for her actions. Unfortunately, the answer lay in his actions five years ago. Actions she could not forget, and memories that even now still caused her acute pain and discomfort. Would she ever be able to move on?

Chapter Four

Lion spent the next week concentrating on Jamie. With Emma stubbornly guarding her secrets and fears, he had little choice. He would have preferred to talk to her, to force her to tell him what those fears were, but each time he tried, she shied away or found something else to do. She was slowly driving him mad.

Jamie had been overjoyed at the first snowfall when he left him at the vicar's home that morning. Lion wondered how much would be accomplished in the day's studies. Rev. Wight, he discovered, was a scholar who enjoyed the time he spent imparting knowledge to his sons and Jamie. The congenial cleric was soft-spoken, but there was an air about him that made people listen when he spoke. Lion liked him immediately and was comfortable with Jamie's education thus far.

Upon his return to the manor, he found Emma in the library looking over some documents. Snow fell beyond the windows behind her, providing a serene winter scene. She looked up when he entered and closed the door. For the past week he'd left her to her own devices, but with the change in weather, he knew some decisions needed to be made.

The first one had to do with their living arrangements.

"I have taken the liberty," he began, "of asking Mrs. Smythe to prepare a room for me."

Her eyes narrowed. "Why?"

"Two reasons," he replied. "I have taken enough advantage of Max and Sarah's hospitality, and with the first snowfall, travel between here and Calderbrooke becomes riskier. I refuse to risk my horses and coachman when there is no need." It would not do to tell her he'd decided he wanted to be closer to her. For now, she seemed to be most comfortable when she thought Jamie was his main focus.

She sighed. "You realize this will cause comment in the area?"

"How?"

"Everyone thinks I'm a widow—"

His laughter burst forth before he could check it. "Emma, you must realize by now with Jamie telling everyone who will listen—and even those who won't—that I'm his father, no one any longer believes you to be a widow. If anything, they are trying to decide when we married without anyone knowing."

She stood and stared daggers at him before turning to the window.

"Unless you want people to believe Jamie was born on the wrong side of the blanket," he continued, "you will have to set aside these unrealistic expectations you have regarding your status."

She whirled to face him. "I almost wish he had been." There was no mistaking the fury in her voice. "Then I could banish you from my life once and for all."

Startled, he nearly stepped back in the face of her wrath. She was shaking, he realized, trying desperately to rein in her emotions. The intensity of her outburst gave him pause. For the first time, a sliver of doubt crept in.

Until now, he'd been confident of his ability to persuade her to return to Edenvale with him. Patience and persistence seemed to be his best weapons. Eventually, she would see that he would not leave her on her own. He'd apparently misjudged the depth of her aversion.

Leaving was still out of the question.

She turned back to the window and stood still as a statue, staring out at the fat flakes falling from a leaden sky.

"You truly never intended to return?" He knew he'd asked the question before, but he couldn't help himself. The thought that she would never have told Jamie about his family, never given him an opportunity to know them, was more than he wanted to believe.

"No."

He waited for more of an explanation. None came. Staring at her blue, wool-clad back, he was reminded of the softness of the skin beneath. Her figure was ramrod straight, but curved in all the right places. He flexed his fingers. What would she do if he threw caution to the wind and got close enough to touch?

"No? That's it?"

She turned to face him. "No, I never intended to return. What else is there to say? I've told you all of this before. How many times do I need to repeat it?"

She looked at him indifferently, as if he was not there. Anger rose in him, but he quashed it. There had to be a way to break through the wall of reserve she'd constructed around herself. He instinctively knew anger wasn't it. Her momentary lapse of minutes ago might never have happened.

"And what of Jamie? What would have become of him?"

"I told you Thomas had already agreed to send him to school. After that..." She shrugged slim shoulders, infuriating him further.

"He is the future Earl of Edenvale. There shouldn't be an 'after that'."

"When I left, I didn't know that," she countered.

What was it about her that kept him on edge? Why didn't he just take Jamie and leave? It would serve her right if he did. Yet he knew he couldn't do it. Not only because he knew it would hurt her and Jamie, but because he would never be able to guarantee she wouldn't retaliate by coming after the boy and disappearing again. Especially now that he was aware of how deep her animosity ran.

"Nevertheless, I told Reverend Wight you thought I perished at Waterloo. Although we both know it's not true, it's a plausible explanation for why you came here as a widow. I'm sure the story has made the rounds by now, and your own servants might be speculating too. Mrs. Smythe made no demur when I asked her to prepare a room."

What was she thinking? Even across the room he could see the ice in her eyes. He took it as a challenge and wondered if he could melt it.

Jamie came home from his lessons in high spirits. He was also soaked from playing in the snow. Remembering what Emma had told him regarding Jamie's tolerance of the cold, Lion took him straight upstairs to get dry and warm.

"It was me and Abel against his brothers," Jamie said. "We had a grand snowball fight."

"Did you win?"

The little boy looked at him with a childish confidence. "Of course. Abel's brothers are too little to get the best of us."

He chuckled as they entered Jamie's room. He'd been surprised not to find Jamie sleeping in the nursery, but Emma merely said there was no need to house him the next floor up all by himself. When they first arrived, she'd kept him with her

59

until she was comfortable with him sleeping alone. Then she'd put him in the room across the hall from hers.

The fire in the grate was banked, but it took no time at all to bring it to life. He grabbed a towel from the washstand then helped Jamie out of his wet clothes. Carl, the footman recently appointed to help Jamie bathe and dress, arrived as Lion was rubbing him down. He left the two of them to finish while he headed for the library. He'd noticed a chess set in there earlier and wondered if Jamie could sit still long enough to learn to play. Perhaps it would work as a distraction this afternoon.

The obviously feminine scrawl on the front of the letter was familiar. Emma hadn't seen it in many years, but she recognized Lion's mother's penmanship. It had been sent over from Calderbrooke with a note from Sarah inviting her for a visit. She glanced out the window. The snow of a week ago was a distant memory, but she knew it was only a matter of time before it returned. She should go spend some time with her friend before winter set in completely. Although not impossible, travel became more difficult once the snow began falling in earnest.

Quickly she penned a reply accepting the invitation to tea tomorrow. She needed to get away from Lion for a bit. Perhaps some space would help her put her thoughts in order. She hadn't dared ask him to leave, but she didn't want him to stay through Christmas. Surely his parents expected him home by then.

With shaking hands, she picked up Lion's letter again. Had he told his mother about her? Was she writing to demand they return? She put the letter down and shook her head. Why did she want to know? And why did she care?

Closing her eyes, she envisioned the countess as she'd last seen her. If anyone could be said to grow old gracefully, it would be Lion's mother. Five years ago, she had still been petite and slim with not a single strand of gray in her dark brown hair. For Emma, she'd been the only mother figure she remembered, and it had been difficult to leave her behind.

Lion entered the library, Jamie on his heels.

"Mama, Papa let me ride on his horse today. It was a long ways up."

Her gaze flew to Lion's, but the question was directed at Jamie. "By yourself?"

"No, I took him up in front of me," Lion answered. "His pony got a stone caught in his hoof while we were out riding, and I couldn't get it out. The poor thing was limping even without Jamie on his back."

"Sam said he would be good as new tomorrow."

She smiled at her son. "Then I'm sure he will."

Jamie came to her side. "What are you doing?"

"I was finishing the list of things that need doing before winter gets here," she replied.

"What's this?" Jamie picked up Lion's letter. "Who is Li-on-el?"

Lion looked up from the chessboard, where he'd been resetting the pieces from his and Jamie's last game.

"That's a letter for your papa," she said. "Would you give it to him for me?"

Jamie, ever curious, asked, "Who is it from?" as he handed it over.

Lion accepted the letter and said, "It looks like it's from my mother—your grandmother."

"Oh," was Jamie's disinterested reply. He began moving the

chess pieces randomly on the board as Lion read.

Emma watched them from behind her desk. Jamie's disinterest was unusual. Until now he wanted to know everything about anything Lion did. Would Lion tell him what his mother had written?

Lion finished the letter and put it down on a side table. He looked at Jamie for a moment before asking, "Do you want to try and play again?"

Jamie looked up. He obviously wanted to ask something, but hesitated. He glanced down at Lion's letter then turned back to the chessboard. For a few minutes there was silence as he continued to play with the chess pieces. Finally, he looked at Lion again and asked, "Does your mama want you to come home now?"

Emma looked down at the papers before her, concealing a smile at the innocent question, but also blinking back the tears at the sadness in Jamie's voice. In a short time, Lion had become so important to Jamie. What would happen when he finally left?

She was concentrating so hard on her own thoughts, she almost missed Lion's reply.

"I think she would like me to, but she didn't actually say so in her letter."

Jamie didn't respond. Lion reached out and stilled the boy's hands on the chessboard and drew him onto his knee.

"Do you want me to go?"

"No, but sometimes you have to go if your mama says so."

Lion mulled this over for a few moments. "I suppose that's true for you, but when you're older you don't always have to do everything your mother says. But"—he held up his hand as Jamie seemed about to speak again—"if I went to visit my mother, would you like to go too?"

Jamie looked up at Emma. Tilting his head to the side, a sign he was thinking, he watched her expectantly. For once, she kept silent, waiting to hear what he would say.

"I think I would like that, but Mama might miss me."

"You don't think she would want to come too?"

"I don't know. Jimmy's mama doesn't like his Nana, so she doesn't go to visit when his papa goes. Sometimes Jimmy and his sisters go, but their mama never goes."

Emma had no notion what Jamie might think about not having grandparents. He knew her parents were dead, and he was fond of his Uncle Thomas, who had been down to see them twice over the past five years. Perhaps, she thought wryly, she should have asked what he thought about his lack of family.

Deep in her own thoughts, she didn't hear Lion's response, and when she looked up, the two were bent over the chessboard discussing moves and strategy. She sighed and made a mental note to talk to Lion about it later.

"My mother sends her love and says to tell you she misses you and Jamie."

Seated before the fire in the library after Jamie was in bed, Lion had just finished reading his letter for the second time while she poured herself a cup of tea. A snifter of brandy sat at his elbow, compliments of the Calderbrooke cellars.

"Nothing to say?" Once again she sensed disapproval in his tone.

"Do you want me to say I miss her too? Because, yes, I do," she replied defiantly.

"But not enough to return to see her."

"No."

"Or to let her know where you went when you left."

"Since you already know that, there is no reason for me to answer."

She felt Lion's gaze on her as she sipped her tea. Forcing herself to relax, she watched him take a large swallow of his brandy.

"Does she want you to return?" She didn't want to ask but, like Jamie, she wondered if he would leave if his mother asked.

"Of course," he replied smoothly, "but since I told her I found you and Jamie, she understands you and Jamie come first. Grace may not, but we will cross that bridge when we come to it."

Unbidden, jealousy rose in her heart, and she spoke before she could still her tongue. "Grace?"

In the act of raising the glass to his lips once more, he stopped and looked at her through astounded eyes. He put down the glass, continuing to stare at her through eyes filled with censure.

"Do you want to know about Grace?"

She shook her head. "No. It's nothing to do with me."

He surged to his feet. "Nothing? Nothing?" His voice rose with each question. "If I didn't know how you felt about Jamie, I would think you didn't have a heart. How can you be so callous?"

"What are you talking about?"

He stared daggers at her for a very long moment before turning away to pace across the room. When he turned back, she could feel his frustration. It nearly overwhelmed her, encroaching on her façade of habitual calm. She closed her eyes, willing herself to be strong. She would not let him affect

64

her.

"What kind of mother are you?"

Startled, she turned to see where he was, nearly spilling her tea in the process. Hastily she put down the delicate china and rose to her feet to face him. Indignation rose and her calm evaporated in an instant.

"I have been a good mother to Jamie," she declared. "I love him more than anything and would never allow him to come to harm."

"And what of Grace?"

She had no idea who he was talking about. She should have asked him what he meant, but the accusation regarding her mothering skills stung. "Grace means nothing to me," she told him, all the while wondering if the woman was his paramour. Maybe she was someone he wanted to marry, but couldn't as long as she was missing. Or perhaps she was the sister or daughter of a friend. Whoever she was, Emma had no interest in hearing about her. For reasons she didn't quite understand, the thought of Lion with another woman made her sick to her stomach.

His eyes glittered in the dim light, anger turning to something deeper, darker. She shivered and, for a moment, tasted fear as he moved closer. He wouldn't harm her physically, of that she was certain, but right now he looked as if he would gladly strangle her and toss her body off the nearest cliff. The thought caused her to step back.

"You have changed, Emma. So much so, I wonder who you really are."

She blinked at the softly spoken words. Where was the fury of moments ago? She stepped away from him, needing breathing space. His size hemmed her in, seeming to sap her energy along with her will. She would not let herself fall prey to

65

him again. Once was enough.

"I have changed." She put the chair between them. "I'm no longer seventeen. I've grown up."

His lips quirked. "I can see that," he murmured as his eyes seemed to strip the clothes from her body. "Unfortunately, you don't seem to have matured."

She bristled at the insult. "Neither have you." Two could play at this game. He still believed the worst of her. It was obvious by the way he looked at her, and the way he questioned her. Yet she knew his physical desire for her wasn't far from the surface.

Unfortunately, neither was hers for him.

Suddenly tired, she turned to go. It was late, and she had things to do tomorrow. She would worry about his accusations another time.

"I'm going to bed. Good night, my lord."

"Perhaps I should join you."

She whirled to face him. "You wouldn't dare!" Would he? A frisson of unease snaked up her spine. She had no defenses against him. Not that it mattered. Men, she knew from bitter experience, took what they wanted regardless of the consequences.

Something in the way she looked at him must have given him pause, for his eyes softened to the texture of mist before he replied, "No, Emma, I wouldn't. I would never forcefully insinuate myself where I obviously wasn't wanted."

She nodded, unable to respond as relief flowed through her. Then she turned and hurried out.

Upstairs in her room, Emma pulled the pins from her hair with shaking fingers. Why did she let him upset her? She could guess what he thought of her, and the scene Lord Owllerton orchestrated had likely reinforced those thoughts. Why couldn't she just ignore him and let him spend time with Jamie?

"I can't think of myself as a viscountess," she told Sarah the next afternoon. "I never wanted a title."

"I was the same way," Sarah said sympathetically. "Max and I were actually wed before he told me about his title."

Emma smiled as she took a sip of her tea. "When Lion and I wed, we were much too young—and he had a healthy older brother. There was no thought of a title in his future."

Sarah picked up a biscuit from the tray and took a bite. After she washed it down with her tea, she said, "I will admit that when I first met you, I thought you too young to have a son Jamie's age. I still do."

Emma put her cup and saucer down on the low table and settled back against the chintz-upholstered pillows at her back.

"I was only fifteen when we wed. Lion was but twenty. We were both much too young to be saddled with such responsibilities." She sighed. "Until Jamie was born, Lion seemed content. But after, he couldn't seem to settle down. I didn't want him to purchase a commission, but I could see that he needed a purpose in his life, something Jamie and I couldn't provide."

"And his brother? Has he told you what happened to him?"

Emma looked out the windows of the small rear parlor Sarah favored. "I haven't asked." And she likely never would. She didn't need to know what happened to Charles. She was just relieved he was no longer able to torment her.

"Will you be going home for Christmas?"

Sarah's question shouldn't have surprised her. At this time

of the year, it was a natural one.

"I wasn't planning on it," she hedged, "and Lion hasn't said anything." At least not specifically about Christmas. "I'm certain I would have heard about it by now if he'd said anything to Jamie."

Sarah's laughter was contagious. "I think the entire county would know by now if he had." Emma could only nod in agreement. "Max is going to miss him, you know. It will be a few years before he can do the same things with David."

Emma didn't contradict Sarah's assumption they might be leaving the area. It would only cause more questions than she was willing to answer right now.

"I would say Jamie will miss Max, but I'm not so certain. Right now, his papa is everything to him." She sighed. "I hadn't realized how very much he wanted a father." She picked up her cup and took a sip of her now-cool tea. "I have been unbearably selfish."

"How so?" Sarah refreshed both cups from the pot.

Emma stared across the room. A portrait of some Calderbrooke ancestor looked down at her from above the fireplace, the woman's dark eyes fixed on a spot somewhere behind her.

"When I first came here, I didn't want to be found. I used my mother's maiden name and swore my brother to secrecy. Lion has visited Thomas twice in the last year alone, asking for news of me, and each time my brother kept his word. He always wrote me to tell me and insisted I should contact Lion, but I wouldn't."

She wished now that her brother had told her of Lion's new status and how Lion's brother met his demise. But, as she'd made it clear she wanted nothing to do with Lion, she supposed he was taking her at her word. And his notes were always short and to the point.

He came by again, asking if I'd heard from you. I told him nothing, but you should write.

A silent sigh escaped. What a contrary creature she was turning into.

She wanted nothing to do with Lion, but now she wished Thomas had told her about him. She couldn't possibly still have feelings for him, but her heart often stuttered when he looked at her, most often over the head of their son. How could she trust someone who had treated her as he had?

"Max is looking forward to visiting Edenvale in the spring," Sarah interrupted her thoughts. "He's never been there, but Lion has assured him the hunting and fishing are not to be missed."

"Lion has always loved to fish. He used to single-handedly keep Cook stocked with the lake or stream's offering of the day." Movement at the window caught her eye, and she nearly laughed out loud at the sight. Jamie went by, Caesar beside him. The pewter-colored wolfhound was nearly as tall as the boy. She hoped he didn't have the dog on a leash, but she couldn't see that. "By the time I was eight," she continued, "I had learned all the best spots on the estate for fishing. Lion's brother couldn't be bothered with us, but I didn't mind. Even then I didn't like Charles much, but Lion practically worshiped his older brother. He always made excuses for him when Charles did something hurtful. He was never convinced it was deliberate." Which was probably why Lion now thought the worst of her.

"Max and his twin were inseparable until Max bought his commission. It wasn't until Max returned injured from Waterloo that he and his brother grew apart. Even then, it took years before Max saw his brother for what he really was. It was

69

disheartening, to say the least." Sarah put down her cup and saucer. "But he has tried to remember his brother in a good light, and has protected his father's memories. I suppose that counts for something."

Emma agreed, but she knew she'd never remember Charles in a good light. Her stomach twisted painfully at the memories she carried of him. Memories that included Jamie falling off a chair the morning after she rebuffed Charles's advances, and other small accidents that seemed to befall Jamie whenever Charles felt slighted. Her throat constricted, and she forced herself to breathe deeply and remember Charles was dead.

Dead, but by no means forgotten. She sincerely hoped he wasn't resting in peace, because she certainly wasn't living that way. He'd made that nearly impossible.

There was a light knock on the door to the parlor, and the butler entered at Sarah's call.

"This just came by special messenger for Lord Lanyon, my lady. However, he is out with his lordship at the moment." He proffered a salver on which rested a creased envelope.

Sarah thanked the butler, took the envelope and passed it to Emma. As the servant left, Sarah suggested he send one of the footmen to the stables to see if the two men could be located. Emma accepted the missive and looked at the writing. An icy shiver slid down her spine.

"I would suggest you open it, but I'm not certain I would in your shoes," Sarah admitted. "I think it best to send someone out to find them. They can't have gone far."

Emma agreed. Especially since she'd seen Jamie in the garden with Caesar less than fifteen minutes ago.

"Can you tell who it's from?"

"This is his mother's writing," Emma told her. "He only received a letter from her yesterday. Another one this soon, and by special messenger, must be urgent."

"I hope it's not bad news."

Emma wondered how it could be anything but.

Chapter Five

By the time she delivered the letter to Lion just before dinner, Emma wished she'd been confident enough to open and read it herself. As it was, Lion merely scanned it without revealing its contents.

When she returned to the library after putting Jamie to bed, Lion was seated before the fire, the letter in one hand, brandy snifter in the other. The brace of candles on the table beside him threw a pool of golden light over him, creating a warm ambience lacking only a dog or cat stretched out before the fire to make it a cozy scene.

She could contain her curiosity no longer. "Is there something amiss?"

He looked up, his eyes dark in the muted light. "My father's not well. He has a weak heart, which the doctor says may fail at any time. My mother writes that he wants to see Jamie."

She didn't know why she was surprised. Hadn't she known having Lion back in her life would change everything? That his very presence would affect not only her, but Jamie? Regardless, however, she knew he did not expect her reply.

"Then you and Jamie should go."

The warm atmosphere of the room dissolved as his regard turned cold.

"Only Jamie and me? You don't think Jamie would want you to come along?"

She turned away, moving toward the window. Pushing aside the drapes, she stared out into the darkness beyond. Whether or not she came along had little to do with Jamie, although she knew if Jamie insisted, she'd go.

"I think you already know the answer to that." Her stomach was already tying itself in knots at the thought.

"I know Jamie would want you to come along, yes, but I am asking whether you would come too."

Did she imagine the terse tone in his voice? Or was it exasperation?

She let the drape fall back into place, blocking out the cold air seeping around the windows, but didn't turn around.

"Would I want to go? No. But if Jamie wouldn't go without me, of course I would." She turned to face him and was startled to find him standing behind her, much closer than she would have preferred. With only the window to step back into, she stood where she was. "I have no wish to go back to Edenvale. I have no objection to you taking Jamie, however."

As if sensing her intention to try to move away, Lion reached out and captured her upper arms, pulling her closer. His warm breath fanned her temples, and when she looked up at him, her gaze involuntarily strayed to his mouth. For one magical moment, she was thrown back in time, remembering the gentle kisses she'd once received from those well-shaped lips. Her heart skipped as she remembered the passion and the tenderness she'd experienced in his arms.

"Why?" Lion's question pulled her out of her far too short daydream. "Why do you harbor such an aversion to the place you grew up? Do you have no good memories of the years you lived there?"

She raised her eyes to his, struggling against the sudden need to feel his arms around her. All she had to do was lean forward. Would he welcome her? Hold her close as he used to? Or would he push her away? She wouldn't take the risk. "I have many," she finally replied. "Unfortunately, they are all overshadowed by the last."

"The last?"

She closed her eyes, unable to continue to meet his. Out of the darkness his face arose, twisted into an expression of distaste. So much for dreams. She opened her eyes to find him looking at her in confusion and...gentleness?

"Do you remember the last thing you said to me?" Her voice shook on the question and tears burned the back of her eyes. She looked away to hide them.

"No."

She shrugged her arms free and stepped away, feeling the window through the drapes at her back. The cool air was welcome as it brought her fully out of her daydream. Slipping around him, she was relieved he did not try to stop her.

"That explains why you have no idea why I never want to return there." And with that, she moved to the door, but stopped and looked back at him as she opened it. "If Jamie insists, I will travel with you to Edenvale, but I will not stay. Once the two of you have been delivered safely, I will continue on to my brother's estate. It is not very far away, and I will be close if Jamie needs me."

Then she stepped through the door and closed it quietly behind her.

Lion ran his hand through his hair. What was wrong with her? Why did she hate the thought of living in the very place she had grown up? He hadn't wanted to believe his brother when he hinted at the same thing. But now, her intractability caused him to wonder if Charles hadn't understood after all.

She hates this place and you too, Charles had told him. *She refuses to return. And she made me swear not to tell anyone where she was.*

He could still hear his brother's gloating voice. Involuntarily, his hands curled into fists. He would get to the bottom of this somehow. He might still miss him, but his brother would not be allowed to control their lives from the grave. Now that Charles was dead, she had no one but him. At least she hadn't turned Jamie against him as Charles had predicted.

The fire beckoned and he returned to his chair. He was tempted to pour himself another brandy, but getting drunk would solve nothing. Resting his head against the back of the chair, he closed his eyes and willed himself into the past.

Scenes flashed against the back of his eyelids. Emma as a child—stubborn, tenacious, but a little bit shy. By the time she was twelve, fearlessness had replaced the shyness. At thirteen, she was gangly and awkward. By the time he'd ridden up the driveway that fateful day during her fifteenth year, he hadn't been home in over a year and a half. His mother's previous letters about how much Emma was growing up had been met with chuckles all around as he enjoyed London in the company of his older brother.

He'd been home three weeks before his life changed irrevocably.

"Will that be all, sir?" the young manservant inquired.

Lion turned from the window, where he'd been staring out at the night. "Yes. Thank you, Liam."

Once the door closed, he turned back to studying the

darkness beyond. Clouds scudded across the moon, thickening until they blocked its light. As the wind picked up, a hint of rain in the air reached him. If Charles didn't come home soon, he was in for a soaking. He shook his head and closed the drapes, turning back to his chair before the fire. He picked up the book he'd been reading on military history and found his place. For a moment he wished he'd gone with his brother into Appleby, but he and Emma had been enjoying their backgammon game so he'd declined his brother's invitation. He had to admit, his mother hadn't exaggerated about Emma growing up. Even Charles had remarked on it when he arrived this afternoon. In a few years she'd be a sensation in London.

He looked down at his book. He'd long had an interest in military history, and now it was about to pay off. His father had agreed to purchase him a commission when he turned twenty-one in a few months. He yawned as the warmth of the fire seeped under his skin. Taking a sip of the whiskey he'd had Liam bring him, he settled down to read about battle strategy during the Wars of the Roses.

A short time later he wasn't sure what woke him, but his start caused the book to slide from his lap and fall to the floor with a thump. The fire was nothing more than glowing coals now, and the rain he'd predicted earlier pelted the window in bursts. He got to his feet and retrieved his book, placing it on the table. Turning down the lamp, he yawned and made his way to the bed.

The door opened suddenly and a figure swathed in white slipped inside, closing the door with a soft click before leaning her forehead against it. Despite the voluminous folds of the garment, there was no doubt the intruder was a woman.

"Emma? What are you—"

"Shhhh." She whipped around, her eyes wide in the

darkness. *"He'll hear you."*

"Who?" he asked in a lowered voice.

"Charles. He's drunk...he came into my room and...and..."

Footsteps sounded in the hall and she bolted across the room. He only had a moment to brace himself before she flung herself against him, her arms locking around his waist.

"Don't let him find me." She was shaking and he put his arms around her, his hand automatically stroking her back in a soothing motion.

As she burrowed closer, he felt her breasts pillowed against his chest, the silk of her hair smelled like herbs, and he realized she really was curved in all the right places.

The door to the library opened and Graves entered, stopping abruptly when he spied Lion seated before the fire.

"Your pardon, my lord. I did not realize you were still in here."

He rose to his feet. "Not to worry, Graves. I was about to retire. Good night."

"Good night, my lord."

As he climbed the staircase, Lion secretly thanked the butler for his intrusion. He didn't need to relive the events of that night or the next few days. He'd been a green youth who had allowed his sudden desire to overcome his common sense. With disastrous results. And while he hadn't used force, he had still been old enough to know better. After all, Emma had been just fifteen, and she'd initially come to him for protection.

It hadn't been a hardship to marry her—until he realized it jeopardized the commission he dearly wanted. Jamie was three months old when he finally wore his father down enough to receive his commission. Another selfish act in a series of selfish actions that left Emma with his parents while he went off to seek the adventure he craved.

Was it any wonder she wanted nothing to do with him now? He'd ruined her life and left her with a child to raise. His parents had been there to help, but he knew she'd needed him. She had been young and insecure. She'd loved him and depended upon him. And he'd walked away.

Perhaps he needn't look any further to find out why she never wanted to return to Edenvale.

Jamie was excited to hear they were going on a trip, although not happy to learn Bobo was to be left behind. By the time he asked for the third—or was it the fourth?—time when they would leave, Emma was ready to tell Lion to take him and go on horseback, and she'd catch up to them later in the coach. She had to remind herself more than once that Jamie had no unpleasant memories of Edenvale and had no idea she was dreading arriving before they even left.

He was too young to understand the nausea she experienced at the very thought of entering the house again, or the cold, clammy feeling that assaulted her when she considered the trip and all it entailed.

The morning they left, it was clear and cold. If it wasn't for the discomfort it would have caused the coachman, she would have wished for rain. At least then the weather would match her mood.

Frost on the trees and in the grass along the road sparkled in the sunlight. The snow of a week ago was long gone, but the frosty nights and early mornings reminded her winter had already made its presence known and would be settling in soon. Her wool cloak was thick and warm, and she made certain they had blankets inside in case Jamie became chilled. She didn't consider herself a coddler when it came to Jamie, having learned much from the vicar's wife about the care and feeding of rambunctious boys, but she knew his tolerance limits.

He would probably fare well at Edenvale. The valley was mild, even for the winters, but the occasional snowstorm might leave its offering for more than a week at a time. By the time it melted completely, the roads would be a muddy, soggy mess. The springtime rains only made it worse, but at least it wasn't very cold.

Once they were moving, Jamie's excitement was impossible to suppress. He kept up a running commentary on everything he could see from the window. Lion indulged him by answering his many questions about their trip.

"It will take us about three days," he told Jamie. And, in response to another question, "I'm certain your grandmother will be surprised at how much you've grown up. She hasn't seen you since you were quite small."

"If it will take so long, where will we sleep?"

"At an inn. I sent Liam ahead with instructions to procure accommodations. Tonight we will stay at the Down & Thistle."

"Oh."

Although she did not participate in the conversation, Emma was not surprised by Lion's forethought. Details had always been important to him. She tried to maintain her interest and focus on the book she'd brought to entertain herself, but she found her attention straying to the conversation between the other two occupants of the coach.

It continually amazed her how patient Lion was with Jamie. She'd always considered herself a patient person, but she knew there were times when she would have become exasperated with all of his questions.

She wondered if someday Jamie might ask her why they had never visited his grandparents, or if Lion had already answered that question. Of course, right now Jamie seemed to take everything in and accept things as they came, but one day he might actually begin to think this turn of events through, and she had no idea what she would say to him then. Would he blame her for keeping him away? Perhaps. But she would never tell him why.

When they reached their stop for the night, she discovered her nervousness over the sleeping arrangements had all been for naught. Lion had his man reserve two rooms. She was not surprised when Jamie, given the choice between sleeping with her or Lion, chose Lion.

Lion had anticipated the possibility and requested adjoining rooms, if they were to be had. The inn was a large and busy establishment. The rooms were clean and comfortable. Jamie stayed close to Lion, all the while taking in everything around him in wide-eyed wonder. They were shown to a private parlor where dinner was served promptly. Once Jamie had eaten, Lion took him upstairs.

He was chuckling when he reentered the parlor a short time later. Emma looked up at him.

"I think he will have a difficult time settling down tonight. He was chattering away at Carl and Liam when I left him."

"He enjoys new sights and watching people," she said. "I think it's a natural curiosity about the world around him."

"He is a fine boy, Emma. You've done well."

She stopped in the middle of lifting her teacup. "I—uh, thank you." She shouldn't be pleased by his compliment. Not after what he'd said to her only a week ago. Yet she was. Absurdly so.

He sat at the table opposite her and poured himself some of

the ale the innkeeper had left. For a time they sat in comfortable silence, each lost in their own thoughts, while the sounds of the inn drifted around them. The noisy public room was a soft drone in the background, the crackle and pop of the fire soothing.

Emma was too aware of Lion, of every shift, every movement. Even as he sipped from his mug of ale, seemingly unaware of her presence, she couldn't help but admire his casual elegance. The rustic surroundings of the inn seemed to magnify his self-assurance. Being so near him, she felt small and insignificant.

"If we continue to have good weather, it will only take us another day and a half instead of three."

She put down her teacup and rested her hands on the table. Her fingers traced the grooves in the rough wood through the worn linen as she looked at him.

"I wrote Thomas to tell him I was coming. I didn't give an exact date."

The silence weighed down on her shoulders. Lion said nothing at first, merely watching her as he sipped his ale. Finally, he put the mug down and folded his arms on the table as he leaned forward.

"Why?"

She didn't pretend to misunderstand and shook her head slowly. "There are too many painful memories I cannot face. Maybe...someday," she offered, "not now."

"Can't or won't?"

She gave him a sad smile. "A little of both, I suppose." She pressed her hands flat against the table, fingers splayed, and took a deep breath. Her heart beat loud in her ears. Could Lion hear it?

"You don't think Jamie will miss you?"

She shook her head. "No. As long as you are there, he will be fine. And Carl will take care of him. He may miss me for a bit, but once he is settled, there will be a new home and grandparents to get used to. He will be fine."

"I see." He emptied his mug, but made no move to refill it. Instead he simply sat there watching her. After a few moments, he reached across the table and covered both her hands with his. They were warm, and she could feel his warmth seeping in through her skin. It was as if he were trying to give her his strength. Strength she did not trust and dared not accept. As she stared into his eyes, she thought she saw regret in the depths before they cleared and he smiled. "I hope someday you will tell me what went wrong."

She pulled her hands from under his and stood. He was too close, and his eyes saw far too much for her peace of mind. Knowing she would tell him someday didn't make it any easier except to understand that somehow she had to make him see what had really happened at Edenvale five years ago. Now, however, was not the time. He was still suspicious of her.

She did not doubt his brother had turned him against her. Hadn't Charles said as much? *He will hate you when he finally returns.* Those words still hurt to think, especially since they had come true.

The next day's intermittent showers had little effect on their progress. Jamie's excitement hadn't dimmed and he once again commanded Lion's attention for most of the way. Only when he finally dozed off for a short time after luncheon did Emma feel the edge of panic she'd been holding back start to encroach.

It had been easier to keep the demons at bay while

interacting with Jamie. Now there was nothing to do except dwell on their impending arrival at Edenvale. A path fraught with emotional danger.

Relax. Easier said than done. Her heart already beat much too loudly in her ears, and her palms might never be dry again. Tomorrow would be much worse. Closing her eyes against the passing fields and villages, she took a slow, deep breath. She would not break down in front of Jamie. Whatever else happened, this trip was for Jamie, and she would not spoil it by falling apart.

Lion shifted beside her, but she didn't open her eyes. Better not to look at him and allow him to see her distress. The coach bumped over something in the road, and her eyes flew open. Jamie slept on the seat across from them covered by a blanket, another folded beneath his head. The jostling hadn't disturbed him.

She glanced over at Lion. A mistake. He was leaning back against the corner where the cushioning met the side of the coach. His broad shoulders were wedged into the corner, arms folded across his chest. Had he not been awake, she might have thought him uncomfortable. Except he was awake—and watching her.

"Is there something wrong?" He kept his voice low, and she appreciated his consideration for their sleeping son.

She shook her head. "No." The single syllable was all she could manage through the tightness in her throat.

Turning back to the window as the coach maneuvered around a farmer with a small wagon, she noted the appearance of the sun.

"You look as if something's wrong."

Emma ground her teeth in frustration and said nothing in return.

Lion said no more, but she could feel his sharp gaze on her. Ignoring him was difficult, and more than once she nearly turned to him. Unfortunately she had no idea what to say.

There was just no easy way to tell him what had really happened five years ago. Not without looking as if she was trying to lay the blame on the older brother he adored. Not that she cared about his brother, but Lion would never believe his brother guilty. Somehow it would all end up her fault.

Tears gathered in response to her thoughts, and she blinked furiously to keep them back. For five years, she'd told herself she didn't care. Not a day passed that she hadn't thought of why she'd left Edenvale and wondered if Lion searched for her. He'd only been back in their lives for less than a month, and she realized how much she cared what he thought. It hurt to think he would blame her. To hear him confirm it would destroy her. Better not to bring up the subject at all.

The next morning seemed promising, with only clouds and a sharp chill to the air. As they traveled farther north, however, the clouds grew heavier and darker until they encountered first rain then snow. By tea time they reached the inn that was their destination for the evening. Lion was thankful he'd considered the possibility of inclement weather in his plans. Only twenty miles from Edenvale, the inn was small, cozy and comfortable. If not for the weather, they wouldn't have stopped at all except to change horses.

It didn't escape his notice that Emma was visibly relieved when they stopped. Her agitation had been obvious all day, and there were dark circles under her eyes, as if she hadn't slept well the night before. Now, however, she seemed to have relaxed, and even responded to Jamie's request for an outing in the snow with, "We'll see what it looks like after we have tea."

Although the snow had been falling steadily for the last hour of their trip, it was by no means a blizzard. By the time they finished tea, however, the wind whipped the heavy snow in every direction. Predictably, Emma did not want Jamie out in such bad weather.

Chapter Six

The storm blew itself out overnight, but left the world covered in white. The quiet accompanying the blanket of snow in the early hours of the morning was peaceful.

His breath misting in the air, Lion trudged through the ankle-deep powder to the stables. The cold stung his lungs as he inhaled the clear air. He didn't mind the cold, nor the short walk. It helped him to order his thoughts.

The snow wasn't deep, and his coachman was familiar enough with the roads between the inn and Edenvale. He knew they would arrive today. His observation yesterday of Emma's relief at halting for the night so near to home had kept him awake far too late last night. Mulling over her plan to leave Jamie with him at Edenvale made him uneasy. It wasn't that he didn't want to introduce his son to his home, but why would she leave Jamie with people who were, for the most part, complete strangers? It made little sense to him, although he appreciated her trust.

The inside of the stables was only slightly warmer, but the odors of horse, sweat, hay and dirt lingered in the air. He found his coachman toward the back with the horses and coaches.

"We'll make it jest fine, m'lord. Jest tell me when ye wants to leave, an' we'll be ready."

Lion did not doubt his coachman's word. They were in

familiar territory. The man likely could get them to Edenvale blindfolded. Yet he hesitated as Emma's face swam before him, green eyes the only color in a bloodless face. Her reticence was one thing, but there was more to her refusal.

And that was what bothered him. There was more to what happened five years ago than he obviously knew. Perhaps even more than what his brother had told him. He had no reason to doubt Charles's word, he reminded himself. Even when he'd wanted to wipe the smug expression off his brother's face, he'd never had reason to believe Charles told him anything but the truth.

"One hour," he said now. "If that changes, I'll send someone out."

He stopped on his way back to take in the bright white landscape as the sun climbed into the brilliant blue of the sky. The mountain peaks of the Lake District gleamed in the distance. A sense of peace, of homecoming, invaded his thoughts. After five long years, he was bringing his family home at last. Emma had once loved this place. And him. He dearly hoped she could do so again.

They would arrive at Edenvale by luncheon. Her brother's estate was another three to four hours beyond. Perhaps one night at Edenvale would convince her. He took a deep breath of the frigid air. He would not give up hope. Then he turned and entered the warm building.

Emma's reluctance to be on their way was obvious. To him. No one else seemed to notice she took her time eating breakfast, or how many times she checked for items she thought she left behind. Once on their way, she retreated into a corner of the coach in silence.

She tried to hide her discomfort, likely assuming he was distracted by Jamie's questions. When they passed through the village of Appleby, she gave up all pretense of reading and closed her book to lean back and close her eyes. The dark curve of her lashes stood out against her pale cheeks, and she gripped her hands together so tightly he was certain the seams along the fingers of her gloves would split from the pressure. He should have asked her why when they were alone, but he did not want to bring her distress to Jamie's attention.

As the coach clattered across the bridge to begin the final drive to the manor, he watched her even as he answered Jamie's questions about the remnants of the walls that used to enclose what was once a very large keep. The fortifications had long since crumbled, but the gatehouse still stood. The small, one-room building of slate and brick was used mostly for storage, but had also been a handy hideout for two boys looking for adventure. He and Charles had spent many days within its walls planning escapades.

Past the gatehouse, they entered a large courtyard. With no need for fortifications, the once mighty curtain wall had been reduced to a three-foot high decorative stone walkway circling the house and gardens. The coach crunched over carefully groomed gravel and rocked to a stop before the large, ironbound front door. The stone steps had already been cleared of last night's snow.

"It's very big," Jamie said, drawing Lion's attention away from Emma's anxiety.

"It is, but you will soon find your way," he reassured him.

A footman exited the house, hurrying to open the coach door and put down the step. Lion climbed out and lifted Jamie down. When he turned back to Emma, she shrank back. Scooting away from the door, she shook her head.

"Emma?"

"I can't. I have to go to Thomas."

"Of course," he replied automatically. "After—"

"No. Not after. Now. I-I must go now."

There was a commotion behind him, and he could hear the harnesses on the horses as they became restless. He hoped Jamie wasn't in the way at the moment because all of his attention was focused inside the coach.

"Emma, don't be silly. You cannot go this very moment. Come along now so the team can be changed."

She continued to stare at him through wide, panicked eyes. Her tension was palpable, and he was afraid she was about to burst into tears.

"Papa!" A high-pitched voice added to the disturbance, and he heard the patter of small feet on the gravel. Moments later he felt a small body latch onto his leg. In resignation, he turned.

Quickly noting Jamie was still standing beside him, he bent down and picked up the little girl and bussed her on the cheek. "Hello, Grace."

Grace looked at him through jade green eyes and asked, "What did you bring me?"

He laughed. "No presents, minx. I brought you a big brother instead."

Lion had no idea how he knew, but as he squatted down and introduced Jamie to five-year-old Grace, he knew Emma had moved back to the door of the coach and was watching them. He wasn't certain how he expected Jamie to react. More than once in the last few weeks, Jamie had told him he wished he had a brother. It might have been easier to tell Jamie before now that he had a sister, but he wasn't confident of his ability to guess either child's reaction to the other one.

Both children managed to surprise him, however.

"Cook made tarts this morning," Grace told Jamie. Taking him by the hand, she urged him to come with her, but Jamie looked to Lion for permission first.

"Cook's tarts are very good, but I suspect it's too close to luncheon for you to have some right now," he told them. "Why don't you take Jamie inside where it's warm and wait for me?"

Grace looked up over his shoulder at that moment, and Jamie grinned. "Look, Mama. Come see."

As he stood and turned to Emma, Lion wondered why he hadn't thought to use Jamie to get her out of the coach. She still had a haunted, panicked look in her eyes, but when he reached for her, she did not shrink back this time. As he took her hand to help her out, he noticed it shook, and once on the ground, she wasn't quite stable. She took a deep breath and let it out slowly. Then she took another.

"Mama, I have a sister," Jamie told her. "Her name is Grace. She has red hair just like you."

"That's nice." The words were forced, and Lion turned to look at her as the coach moved off. She held herself stiffly, her eyes watching the coach until it turned around the end of the manor toward the stables.

"Emma?" His voice seemed to startle her, and she jerked her head back as she turned to him.

The long, slow breaths had changed, and she was nearly gasping for air. Wrapping her arms around herself, she continued to take short, staccato breaths. The pulse at her throat beat violently, and a sheen of moisture beaded her upper lip.

"Can we go inside now?" Jamie asked. "I'm cold."

Emma's eyes widened further. The earlier, panic-stricken

look returned. She began to tremble, whether from the cold or something else, he wasn't sure.

"No," she whispered. Lion was thankful only he heard her. "I can't. Have to—"

"Grace, why don't you take Jamie inside to Nana? We'll be inside in a moment."

He didn't know if both children believed him or not. He never took his eyes from Emma. After a moment, he heard the sound of feet on the gravel, then on the stairs. Once the door closed, he reached out to steady her.

"What's wrong? What are you afraid of?"

"I-I'm n-not afraid." The response was automatic, the lie obvious. She looked around. "Wh-where is th-the coach? Wh-why hasn't it re-returned yet?"

"I didn't tell it to return." He slid his arm around her waist and attempted to steer her toward the door. "Come, we can discuss it inside." She wouldn't budge.

"No. I-I told you. I can't."

"Can't? Or won't?" It was difficult not to lose his temper, but she was acting no older than Grace. "Come, Emma. Cease this nonsense and come inside."

She shook her head again, this time hard enough her bonnet was in danger of falling off. Wrenching herself away from him, she stumbled and nearly fell before righting herself.

"I told you. I can't. I won't."

He stalked after her, spinning her around to face him when he caught up with her. Holding her by the shoulders, he shook her.

"You'll come inside and—"

"And what?" she asked, struggling against his hold. "Or what?" She twisted, trying to break away, but he merely moved

91

his hands to her upper arms and tightened his grip. "Let me go." The demand was little more than a growl.

He shook her again. "No. Either you come inside on your own or I will carry you."

This time there was no mistaking the look of terror in her eyes. Nor was there any doubt she would not go willingly. Gasping for breath, she tried to push him away. When he stilled her hands, she kicked him. When fighting didn't work, she turned to pleading.

"Please don't." Her voice was ragged. "I can't." He was not proof against the fear in her eyes, no matter how much he wanted to ignore it.

"Why?" He tried gentling his voice. "What are you afraid of? And don't tell me you're not."

She shook her head. "I can't. Talking about it only makes it worse. Have to go away."

"Not until you explain. I don't want to have this conversation outside. We can discuss it inside where it is warm." As he pulled her to him, holding her close against him to soothe her as well as ward off any further attacks, she continued to squirm against him. "I don't mean to hurt you, Emma. Surely you know that?" Her response was to continue fighting.

Finally, she seemed to give up. Sagging against him, she looked up at him with tormented eyes and asked in a tortured whisper, "Why do you hate me so?" Then her eyes rolled up into her head, and she went limp.

He lifted her, holding her close for a moment before looking down into her white face. Hate her? How could she think he hated her? His heart squeezed painfully in his chest. There were times when he did not trust her. The day he'd returned home after delivering some dispatches had shattered his trust.

He remembered little about that day. Mid-April was more often than not pleasant, so it probably hadn't been overcast or raining. She had come outside to meet him as he prepared to dismount. The disturbing letter he'd received from his brother was the only reason he'd made the long trip home on such short notice. He wanted to see for himself. The sight of her standing at the top of the stairs, unmistakably pregnant, was seared into his memory. He never even entered the house that day, and if either of them spoke, the memory had been washed away later when he stumbled into a pub in Appleby and proceeded to get roaring drunk.

Hate her? No. Despite attempts to erase her from his memory, he hadn't been able to. He'd torn Carlisle apart, convinced she wouldn't go far from her brother's protection. When she couldn't be found there, he'd looked farther afield to Edinburgh. Despite making a number of trips to London while looking for information for Max, it had never occurred to him that she would travel that far south. He'd even hired the Scottish equivalent of a runner to scour the highlands. And all the time she was living in Max's backyard. He wished now that he'd attended Max's brother's funeral. By the time Christmas of 1817 came around, his attempts had become half-hearted. And since her brother continued to deny knowing her whereabouts, he'd all but given up. Then Charles died.

That was three years ago. He'd stepped up his search for her, but even then it was only to ensure Jamie was not cheated of his inheritance. He wasn't convinced he wanted her back until he walked into the Calderbrook drawing room and found himself face-to-face with her again. The memories returned in a rush, and he wanted nothing more than to spirit her away and tie her to his side. Even the indiscretion with Owllerton hadn't changed his mind, except to remind him she couldn't be trusted. That she was no better than other wives of the *ton* who strayed once the requisite heir appeared. At least he knew Jamie was his.

The sharp smell of hartshorn awakened Emma. She rested on something soft, but could see little in the dim light of the room. Moving her head away from the unpleasant, acrid odor, she closed her eyes again.

"Emma?"

Lion's voice was gentle and she turned toward the sound, opening her eyes.

"What happened?"

"You fainted."

"I never faint."

Lion chuckled. "Then I'm honored to be the first person into whose arms you have fainted."

She sat up abruptly, regretting it instantly as her head began to spin. Lion reached out to steady her.

"Where am I?"

He hesitated and her memory returned. Her eyes took in the furnishings. Even the dim light filtering through the drapes could not hide the familiarity of the room. Her throat tightened and panic rose.

"Wh-why did you bring me here?"

"I thought to give you some privacy."

She shifted her feet to the floor and made to rise. "Th-thank you." The rug was soft under her feet and she looked around. "Where are my shoes?"

"In the dressing room," he replied.

She rose and started in that direction then stopped and

turned back. "I'm ready to go now. Could you have the coach brought around?"

She heard him sigh as she entered the dressing room. The sight that met her eyes stopped her cold. Her trunks sat in the middle of the room, the top of one opened. Her half boots sat beside one of them. Picking up the footwear, she stalked back into the bedroom.

"What are my trunks doing in there? It looks as if someone was about to unpack them."

The words were forced through the tightness in her throat. Crossing the room to the bellpull, she yanked on it then sat in a nearby chair to put on her shoes.

"Emma," he began, "you can't possibly expect—"

The door opened and a maid entered. She looked from Lion to Emma, unsure who to address. Emma solved the problem for her.

"Please have the coach brought around," she said quickly. Her throat was still tight, and her heartbeat thundered in her ears. "And...and send someone up for my trunks."

Before the maid was able to leave, however, Lion intervened. "Do not do any such thing, Jenny. Go back to your duties."

The maid's eyes widened at the hard tone in his voice, and she dropped a quick curtsy before hurrying from the room.

"You can't do that," Emma cried. "I need to go. Thomas is waiting for me." Her palms were sweaty, and she had to concentrate on her bootlaces to get them properly tied.

Lion merely watched her finish lacing up her boots before replying, "I just did. Your brother will not be worried over one day's delay."

She jumped to her feet and swayed as the room became a

blur. Closing her eyes, she counted to five then opened them. Lion still stood beside the chaise she'd awakened on, but she ignored him. Her cloak hung on a peg near the door. Hurrying to it, she snatched the cloak down and ran out into the hall and down the staircase.

Lion caught up to her as she was opening the front door.

"Where are you going?" he demanded as she pulled it open.

She didn't answer. Now was not the time. She had to get out of the house. Before she broke down again. The constriction in her throat tightened further, cutting off her air. Spots formed before her eyes, and she concentrated on breathing.

Once outside, she didn't hesitate. She ran. The cold air stung her cheeks and caused her eyes to water. Still she ran. A sharp pain developed in her side, but she refused to stop. Nothing would stop her from putting as much distance between herself and Edenvale as she could.

It was still early enough in the day that the sun shone brightly from a cloudless sky. She slowed as she reached the bridge, the pain in her side having intensified. Gasping for breath, she leaned against the pillar at the end of the bridge and turned to look behind her. Half expecting to see Lion following her, she relaxed as she took in the empty drive.

Her heartbeat gradually returned to normal, and her breathing slowed to a manageable pace as she looked around her. With the sun out, the snow was melting rapidly, leaving brown spots among the undulating white landscape. Her gaze returned to Edenvale, the gray stone-and-slate roof standing out against the brilliant blue of the sky. She sighed.

The worst had come to pass. For months after she left five years ago, she contemplated returning. Every time, however, she would experience acute terror at just the thought. On one occasion, she'd tried to come back. Leaving Jamie at Englevyn with Thomas, she had gotten as far as Appleby before her heart began racing. By the time they reached the bridge she stood beside now, the terror had returned, and she'd ordered the coachman to turn around and take her back. That was the last time she'd even considered coming home.

Home. Edenvale had always been home, and she loved it. Even now, looking at it in the distance brought bittersweet memories of her childhood and adolescent years. If not for Charles, she would never have left. And if not for Charles, she could return. Now, however, she knew she couldn't. The memories, the terror, the pain wouldn't let her.

Fresh tears sprang to her eyes as she realized she was forever barred from the one place in the world she should have felt safe—and from the only family she really had.

Turning her back on Edenvale, she trudged across the bridge toward Appleby. Her reticule still rested in the small pocket inside her cloak. She was not completely destitute, but she had no idea how much it might cost her to either hire someone to take her to Carlisle and Thomas or for a ticket on the stage.

By the time she reached the town, she was tired and hungry. The coaching inn didn't seem busy so she stepped inside, hoping the McKenzies were still the owners. Her luck held as a young woman came through a door from the back and noticed her.

"Can I help you, miss?"

The woman was fair-haired and slim, her eyes dark in the dimness of the room. She looked familiar.

"Miss Emma?"

Emma looked closely. "Sally?"

The woman nodded, a wide smile breaking out on her plain face. "What are you doing here? Have you come back to stay?"

Emma didn't know what to tell her. "I've brought Jamie to see his father." It was a safe enough statement. "Right now, I'm famished. Do you...could you...?"

"Oh, where are my manners? You come right back here." She led Emma into the back hall and into a private parlor where a cheerful fire blazed. "I just put on a big pot of stew, so it won't be ready yet, but I have some pickled trout and fresh bread. I'll bring you a pot of tea. You look like you could use it. Make yourself comfortable. I'll be right back."

After she left, Emma let out a long breath as she glanced around the small, neat room. Sally had once been the cook's assistant at Edenvale. Only a few years older than Emma, she would slip Emma a tart or scone when Emma occasionally ventured into the kitchen. The two had become friends of a sort, but she knew how much Sally liked to chatter. If her luck held, she wouldn't have to say much, but Sally could tell her what she wanted to know.

Emma removed her cloak and spread it over a chair before the fire. The hem was soaked, and there were spots of mud on it. Seating herself in the other chair, she held her feet out toward the warmth.

Staring into the flames, her thoughts went to Lion and Jamie—and Grace.

They, probably Lion's mother, had named her baby Grace. No wonder Lion questioned her mothering instincts. Grace wasn't his paramour, or a friend's daughter or sister. She wasn't even *his* daughter.

No, she's yours, her conscience needled her. *Your daughter. And you walked away.* Lion's words came back to haunt her. *What kind of mother are you?*

For the first time in five years, shame washed over her at what she'd done. She'd left a helpless baby. An infant who wasn't to blame for its parents' actions. She'd turned her back on her own flesh and blood. It didn't matter that she knew Lion's mother and Mousey, her former nursemaid, would take care of her. It didn't matter that Charles seemed to have no interest in the baby, either. She had rejected her own child and abandoned her. If she needed a reason for Lion to hate her, she'd found it.

Sally reentered the room, interrupting her unhappy thoughts.

"Here you go, Miss, I mean, m'lady." She put a tray down on the table in the center of the room.

Emma levered herself up out of the chair as Sally began setting out plates of food, a teapot and cup with saucer. "Do you no longer work at Edenvale, Sally?"

Sally looked up and paused for a moment before continuing to set plates of food on the table. "Oh no! I married Ian McKenzie three years ago. When his mum died near two years ago, we moved in to help out his pa, an' I was glad to do it. Since none of his sisters and brothers have any interest in the inn, his pa turned over the running of it to us. It got me out of the big house an' that's been good."

Emma seated herself at the table and poured herself a cup of steaming brew.

"It's good it is to see you, Miss, I mean, m'lady," Sally continued. "Her ladyship was so worried about you when you left, but she fair doted on little Grace. And she missed Master Jamie something fierce, but she said you'd come back. And here you are."

If Sally thought it odd Emma had walked into the inn alone, she didn't show it. Instead she continued to chatter about the happenings in the town over the last few years as she set out a spread Emma was certain she wouldn't do justice to.

"There." Sally stood back, hands on her hips. "Now you eat up. Do you need anything else?"

"When does the next stagecoach come through on the way to Carlisle?"

"Tomorrow. Are you expecting someone?"

"No-no, I'm not expecting anyone." Sally waited for her to explain. "I—" She hesitated a moment while she took a sip of hot tea, giving herself the courage to continue. "I need to get to my brother's home. I hate to ask it of you, but might I have a room for the night?"

Bless her, Sally didn't hesitate.

"Of course, Miss, I mean, m'lady. I keep forgetting you're a viscountess now after Master Charles's death. That was a sad time, it was. Her ladyship was never the same. Master Lionel, I mean His Lordship, was very sad for a long time too. I think he thought it his fault his brother died. But it wasn't, you know. It was because his brother was drinking and talking about y—" She stopped abruptly and clapped her hand over her mouth. "Forgive me, m'lady. You know I talk too much and sometimes I just rattle on and—"

"It's all right, Sally. I didn't know about Charles's death until a month ago when my husband told me. I've been living in the south for the past few years." It wouldn't do to give Sally too many details. She was a nice person, but a chatterbox with no real control over her tongue. When she worked at Edenvale, the cook had always told her someday her tongue would get her into trouble if she didn't have a care.

"I-I will just go and make sure we have a clean and aired room for you."

Then she hurried out of the parlor, leaving Emma to eat and think—in silence.

Helping herself to some pickled trout, she sighed in delight as the sharp, tangy flesh practically melted on her tongue. Of all the things she missed, the local specialty was one near the top of the list. Sally had obviously learned something in the kitchen at Edenvale.

Emma had moved back to the chair before the fire by the time Sally returned for the dishes. She had been hungrier than she thought and nearly cleaned every plate. Now she was a little drowsy, but did not want to fall asleep so early in the day.

"Sally, would you tell me what you meant earlier? About Lion feeling responsible for Charles's death."

"It was on account of the things he said about you, m'lady."

"About me?"

Sally began stacking dishes on the tray.

"Mmm-hmm. It wasn't long after Twelfth Night, and there was lots of snow. They had both been drinking with some of the townsfolk, but then his lordship said something about you, and Master Lion told him to take it back."

"Do you know what he said?"

Sally shook her head. "My Ian told me about it later, but he didn't remember what was said, only that Master Lion called him a liar and tried to hit him, but his lordship pushed him down and laughed at him. Then Master Lion left, but his brother stayed. Ian offered him a room later so he wouldn't have to ride out so late, but he left anyways. Menfolk can be stupid sometimes." She picked up the tray and turned to leave the room.

"What happened to him?"

"Froze to death. Someone found him on the road just the other side of the bridge the next day. I know we shouldn't talk bad about the dead, but I don't miss him. He wasn't a nice man." She paused and shook her head, then continued, "Your room's ready. I'll be back in a minute to show you up."

Then she left.

Chapter Seven

Lion stood at the library window. The sun reflecting off the patches of melting snow nearly blinded him, but he couldn't move. With his gaze firmly glued to the gatehouse and driveway, he expected Emma to reappear any moment. But she didn't. And as the clock on the mantle behind him ticked away the minutes, his anxiety rose.

He was comforted by the thought that it was not snowing. Not like the night he'd left Charles at the coaching inn in Appleby. The day was still cold, and if a breeze came up it would be bitter. But not as cold as that January night. Nor as bitter as the taste of regret in his mouth. His father hadn't blamed him.

"He was a man," his father said. "It was not your fault he exercised poor judgment and refused McKenzie's offer of a room."

It hadn't mattered. Lion knew he shouldn't have left Charles. So what if Charles had made him angry? So what if Charles had made him look like a lovesick fool? Charles was his brother. And he'd known Charles was drunk.

Emma was his wife. He had promised to love, honor and cherish her. At twenty he'd loved her. Five years ago, he thought he'd erased her from his thoughts. He hadn't. More than that, he was beginning to suspect he still loved her.

He should have gone after her immediately. She couldn't have outrun him. His anger at what he considered foolishness and irrational hysterics kept him back. He'd turned and stormed back into the house. If she refused to be inside where it was warm, he would not force her. She'd return eventually.

But she hadn't.

And now he stood watching for her, undecided as to what he should do.

A part of him wanted to go find his mother and ask her what she knew about the reason Emma left. With his father still abed, he didn't want to disturb him with questions. As soon as he was better, however, he'd ask him as well. But right now he couldn't abandon his post. Not while there was the possibility she might come back.

The door behind him opened, and he turned to see the butler crossing the carpet, a silver salver in his hand.

"This just arrived for you, my lord," he said as he proffered the tray, on which rested a slightly crumpled folded piece of paper.

"Thank you, Tuttle." He unfolded the missive and scanned the few lines. "Is there someone waiting?" he asked the retreating butler.

"I believe so, my lord. Shall I check?"

"Yes, but if someone is waiting, you may tell them to leave. I will see to the delivery myself."

After Tuttle left, Lion looked down at the note again. Had his relief been obvious to the butler upon reading Emma's request for her trunks and maid to be sent to Appleby?

At least now he knew she was somewhere warm and dry. He would honor her request, although not in the way she likely expected.

The interior of the coaching inn hadn't changed. The rough-hewn tables and benches were still lined up in straight rows, with cozy booths lining one wall. When occupied, the booths were lit with only one small candle, allowing the occupants anonymity if they wished it. The low beams on the ceiling still held tallow candles, which added to the smoky interior when the room was full.

He had deliberately waited a full half hour after Emma's maid and trunks were delivered before arriving.

Sally McKenzie bustled out of the back, her fair hair braided and wrapped around her head in a coronet.

"It's good to see you again, milord," she greeted him cheerfully. "If you're looking for Em—I mean, Her Ladyship, she's in the room at the top of the stairs."

"Thank you, Sally."

Emma was standing at the window, her back to the door, when he entered at her answer to his knock. Without turning, she said, "I really didn't need anything more, Mary."

He cleared his throat and she whirled around.

"Oh! I thought you were—"

"I know."

"What do you want?" The hint of suspicion in her voice reminded him of their last parting only a few hours ago. Did she think he'd come to force her back?

"I came to talk to you." Her eyebrows inched upward as he closed the door. "What should I tell Jamie when he asks why you left without saying goodbye to him?"

The question took the wind out of her, and she sat down heavily on the side of the bed. He looked around and, spying a

105

chair near the fireplace, crossed to it and sat as well. And waited. She wrestled with herself for a moment before looking at him, embarrassment and guilt in her eyes.

"I don't know." She put her hands up to her cheeks, holding them there for a moment before returning them to her lap. Then she sat up straight and looked him in the eyes, her own having frosted over. "It wouldn't be a problem if you had kept your promise."

"What promise?"

"To send me to Thomas. I told you before we started this journey I couldn't stay at Edenvale. Did you think to force me to do so?"

He managed to mask his own chagrin behind surprise. Yet she was right. He had assumed one night would not be a problem. That maybe one night would turn into two, two into three and so on. He hadn't considered that she would be terrified of staying there.

"I didn't think one night would hurt," he confessed. "I would have sent you on to your brother tomorrow."

She looked at him in disbelief then shrugged her shoulders. "It matters not now."

As he watched her, he was struck by her vulnerability. Fear and uncertainty wrapped around her like a cloak, despite the brave front. Now that he understood her fear was real, he was unsure how to approach it. Did it mean she would never return to Edenvale? There were other properties she could live on, but was her fear of his home or the people inside?

"I will have the coach here for you in the morning. If we leave early enough, I should be back by dinner time. I don't think Jamie and Grace will miss me for one day."

She wanted to argue with him. He could see it in her eyes. She did not want his company. It was too damn bad. He would not allow her to travel alone, even with a coachman and footman for protection. When she spoke, however, the topic was completely unexpected.

"I owe you an apology," she began. "About Grace..."

"What about Grace?"

She worried the material of her dress. Pleating it and unpleating it over her lap, she continued hesitantly. "I-I didn't know."

"Didn't know what?"

"I didn't know what they named the baby. So I—"

"So you had no idea who I was speaking about when I questioned you about her."

She shook her head.

"And how is it you didn't know your own child's name?" He was finding this conversation bizarre. Grace was one of her own names. Surely she'd been asked.

"I left."

Her voice had gone soft, and he moved his chair closer to hear her. When she didn't seem to notice, he gave up trying to stay removed and sat beside her. She looked up at him, her eyes swimming with tears. He resisted the sudden urge to pull her into his arms.

"I left," she repeated. "I never even held her. I didn't want—"

Shocked at what he was hearing, he interrupted her. "You left? What do you mean, you left? When?"

She sniffed and wiped her eyes. "I left. A fortnight after she was born. The doctor told your mother I needed a change of scenery. The baby was too young to travel."

Did he dare ask why she never returned to claim Grace? Or why she hadn't given the baby a name during the fortnight

107

before she left?

"Yet you never thought to write and ask about her?"

"I didn't want to be found. Once I left my brother's. I just wanted to forget."

"Forget what?"

She looked up at him for a long time. He thought he glimpsed regret in her eyes, but the moment passed. The knock on the door startled them both, and she jumped from the bed as if scalded. Hurrying to the door, she threw it open as he stood and walked to the window.

"I brought you some hot water." Her maid's voice came from the open door.

"Thank you, Mary." Was that relief he heard in Emma's voice?

Behind him he heard the maid enter and set down whatever she carried. He felt rather than heard Emma approach. She stopped beside him and said in a low voice, "You should tell Jamie I have already left for my brother's. I spoke to him last evening when we stopped. If he believes I left after he went in the house, he may ask why I didn't say goodbye, but he knew I did not plan to stay at Edenvale. Unless he saw you bring me inside, he might very well think I left with the coach."

"And Grace?"

She hesitated before she answered. "She does not know me. Why should she care?"

He turned to look down at her. The light from the window turned her pale skin nearly transparent, and he knew a sudden urge to reach up and caress her cheek. "I think the question should be why don't *you* care?"

She turned away. "I think you should go now. I will be ready in the morning."

Short of trying to force her to answer, there was little he could do with her maid in the room. He was certain the woman, unlike Jenny, would not leave unless Emma gave the order.

He walked to the door and paused to turn and look back at her. In the waning light of the window, there was a sadness about her that touched him. Despite his mistrust and reservations about her, she was still his wife. He still owed her his protection and support. If that was all she'd accept for now, then that's what he would give. Their conversation had given him food for thought. For now, it was progress. "I will come for you at eight."

Outside in the hall, he stood for a moment, thinking over their conversation. As he headed down the stairs, he shook his head. How many other lies had Charles told him?

Emma stared at the closed door. *Why don't you care?*

She shivered at those words. Words that condemned her as surely as she deserved. It did no good to tell him she hadn't known. That before today, Grace had been a shadowy, unnamed figure she'd only wanted to forget. Seeing her, knowing her name, hearing her voice, had made her all too real.

The sound of rustling reminded her she wasn't alone, and she turned to Mary with a smile.

"Thank you for the water. It might have been nice to have a bath, but this will do until we reach my brother's home tomorrow."

"Mrs. McKenzie said she'd have a tray sent up, or you could have the parlor again."

It was still early, but suddenly the day caught up with her, bringing with it exhaustion, both mental and physical.

"I will have a tray in my room and an early night." Despite her fatigue, she doubted sleep would come easily.

Keeping herself busy as she washed and readied for bed, she tried not to think of Lion's parting words or their conversation. It had been a surprise to him that she hadn't known the child's name. More damning, however, was the sentence he'd cut off. One she hadn't bothered to finish after he'd done so. *I didn't want her.*

After watching him with Grace, she knew that was something else she could never tell him. It was obvious he'd grown attached to the little girl. Was it because Grace was Charles's daughter? Or had he taken pity on the child?

She shook her head. Under the law, Grace was his because she was born to his wife during their marriage. It was all that truly mattered. Whether he would ever forgive her for abandoning her daughter, she refused to speculate on.

Mary hung her traveling dress over a chair and helped her into a warm, flannel nightgown and thick velvet robe. She glanced around the room as Mary built up the fire with the wood beside the fireplace. There was no dressing table, so she sat in the chair Lion had used in front of the fireplace. After the maid removed the pins from her hair, Emma took the brush in an effort to give herself something to do.

Mary left, taking the traveling dress and promising to have the mud brushed from it and the dress ready to wear by morning. Unfortunately, she left Emma to her thoughts. Thoughts that weren't being nice to her at the moment.

She didn't blame Lion for not understanding. She should have told him why the doctor suggested a change of scenery. Would he have understood her listlessness? Her inability to do anything, even eat? Would he scoff at his actions as being to blame for her melancholy after Grace was born?

She sighed. Even his mother hadn't made any effort to understand. Of course, his mother was blind when it came to Charles. In her eyes, he could do no wrong. After all, he was the heir. The one time she attempted to tell her mother-in-law of Charles's advances, the countess had merely told her to lock her door. The dismissive tone from the only mother figure in her life had been a severe blow. She never bothered to explain that locking the door hadn't deterred Charles.

Pulling the brush through her curls occupied her hands. She wished it could also occupy her mind. It was too easy to become lost in thought, reliving memories she'd managed to suppress over the last five years. With Lion's advent into her life again, remembering seemed to be all she did. And with the memories, she relived the pain.

Mary returned with a tray, interrupting her dismal thoughts.

"I'll be back in a bit with a pot of tea, m'lady. Mrs. McKenzie had just put on the kettle when I came down for your tray."

Emma plaited her hair and tied it off with a ribbon. She was tired and drowsy. A light meal and some tea would be just the thing to help her calm down and, hopefully, sleep.

Lion bided his time until after dinner. With Jamie and Grace finally in bed, he and his mother ate in the small family dining room. Unfortunately, with the servants present, they could only talk of the mundane. Once the dessert had been served, he sent the servants away and turned to his mother. Impatient, he got right to the point.

"Do you know why Emma originally left Edenvale?"

"The doctor insisted she needed a change of scenery."

"Why? Did the birth not go well?"

His mother colored, and he realized that childbirth was one of those topics seldom discussed in mixed company. Yet he needed answers and he doubted his father could tell him what might have happened in the room when Grace was born.

"It went perfectly well," she replied stiffly. "'Twas not particularly long, and everything went very smoothly."

"I see." But he didn't, and he didn't know which questions to ask. "Then why did Emma need a change of scenery if all went well?"

"She was despondent. Even before Grace was born, some days she would just lay abed. She seemed to be tired constantly, but she wouldn't eat. And she cried all the time." His mother sighed. "Mousey tried everything, but she could only coax Emma into eating occasionally."

"Was she this way the entire time she was increasing?" he asked. "I don't remember her being like that before she had Jamie."

"On and off, yes. But mostly it was the month or so just before Grace was born. I hired a wet nurse because I was afraid she would be too weak to nurse Grace like she did Jamie. Thank goodness I did." She gave a delicate shudder, and Lion was reminded of her disapproval after Jamie was born when Emma insisted on nursing Jamie herself.

Lion watched his mother cut up a pear into small pieces then spear one and put it in her mouth. She seemed so completely unconcerned that he wondered if she was hiding something. Did she know something, or was she truly as ignorant of the facts as she seemed?

He took a sip of his wine then tried to bring the subject back to what he wanted to know. "Did you know Emma is terrified of staying here?"

That got his mother's attention. She put down her fork and turned soft, gray eyes on him. "No, I didn't. What is she terrified of? Is that why she stayed away for so long?"

"If I knew what frightened her, I would know how to deal with it." He drained his wine glass and set it down. "What about Grace's father? Did she ever mention him?"

He'd told himself he'd never ask about the unknown man, but right now he needed answers more.

His mother shook her head. "She refused to say. The one time I pressed her she became hysterical and said it was all my fault. The only person who seemed to be able to talk to her was Charles. They were very close."

That was the last thing he wanted to hear. If what Charles wrote in his letters was any indication, Emma had told him far more than she should have. Charles might not have said anything to their parents, but he made certain Lion knew what was going on.

On the other hand, Charles had told him Emma insisted on naming the baby Grace before she disappeared. Something he now knew to be false.

How much then was actually true? He wished he hadn't burned the letters. Confronting her with Charles's letters might have persuaded her to tell him the truth.

"He was so good with Jamie. Do you know she tried to keep Jamie away from Charles? I put a stop to that."

"How?"

"I reminded her Jamie was his nephew. There was no reason to keep him away. He wouldn't let Jamie come to harm."

"And how did she react?"

The countess finished off her pear before she replied. "She wasn't happy. She insisted Jamie was too small for Charles to take care of properly. I don't know why she would have thought that, but she was extremely overprotective with Jamie. I suppose in her place, I might have been the same."

"Why?"

Taken aback, she repeated his question. "Why? Because Jamie was all she had. Despite your unconventional marriage, Emma loved you. If you hadn't come home from the war, Jamie would have been all she had left of you."

The morning arrived entirely too early for Emma. A fitful night's rest, punctuated by unpleasant dreams, left her irritable and cross, and she took pains not to take her ill temper out on Mary. Lion, however, was a different matter. Especially since he greeted her cheerfully, looking well-rested and as if he hadn't a care in the world.

"I trust you slept well."

Emma winced at his too-cheerful tone. Her response closely resembled a grunt as she entered the carriage, disdaining the help of his hand. She didn't want his company and would have preferred to make this trip alone. If he insisted on accompanying her, he should not be surprised if she was uncommunicative. She deliberately took the seat with her back to the horses so as not to sit beside him.

"My parents send their love," he said as the coach began to move. "And their hope you will come back to visit them. Soon."

She pressed her lips together, but could not continue her rude behavior. "I wish I could." There were times being a lady was detrimental to her state of mind.

"Why not? What is it about Edenvale that makes you afraid to even enter it?"

"I—" She could not give voice to her fears. Even with Charles gone, the house still held memories of the terror she'd been subjected to by him. Terrors that had resurfaced in her dreams the night before. There was no logical reason to explain her fear—not with the knowledge that Charles could no longer harm her. She fell silent.

Lion shifted in his seat, staring out the window for a long time before he turned back to her. Her hackles rose beneath his piercing stare then wavered as his gaze grew soft.

"Needless to say, Grace is curious about you. There was no end to her questions last evening until I promised to bring her to Englevyn one day to see you."

Her curiosity was piqued. "Why?"

"Why what?"

"Why would you make such a promise?"

"Because it was a reasonable request."

She wasn't certain she saw it the way he did, but chose not to pursue that line of questioning.

"She's our daughter, Emma," he said tightly, "even if you refuse to recognize it."

"She's not—"

Lion's hands shot out and clasped her upper arms in a punishing grip. Her head snapped up. For a moment she feared he would harm her, so dark were his eyes. His lips thinned, and when he spoke it was with menacing intent.

"You will never, *ever* imply that she is anything other than *our* daughter." The very softness of his voice did more to instill fear in her than the loudest shouting had ever done. "Should you ever consider doing so, know that I will cut you from our lives and leave you to your brother's charity."

When he let go of her, she sank back against the plush

115

cushions. Unable to speak over the constriction in her throat, she closed her eyes to blank out his face and the nearest she'd ever come to seeing outright hatred in his eyes.

"If you do not wish to become acquainted with her, you need only say so."

She opened her eyes. His face was in shadow opposite hers, but she knew he studied her all the same. She looked away, blinking back tears.

"I did not say so." It was all she could say and not reveal her emotions.

The silence between them grew. She resisted the impulse to squirm in her seat and kept her mouth firmly closed. After a few minutes, she heard him sigh over the rumbling of the coach.

"She's only a child, Emma. She is not responsible for how she came to be here."

Emma swallowed a lump in a painfully dry throat. It was easy for him to say that. He hadn't been the one subjected to unwanted intimacy. The one who carried an unwanted child for nine months. And he wasn't the one who had been driven from the only home he'd ever known in order to preserve his sanity.

On the other hand. "I know." She did not blame Grace for her existence. Yet Emma was worried. Would she ever be able to look upon her daughter and not remember the how and why of her conception?

Having seen her, Emma was glad the child did not resemble Charles. Had that been the case, she was not certain of her acceptance.

"She is a lot like you at the same age. Fearless. Irrepressible. Curious. She took to Jamie instantly. And in the event you were concerned, Jamie never asked about you until bedtime. And then I'm certain it was because Grace asked about you first."

Curiosity had long been a trait she no longer indulged in, but the thought that Grace wanted to know more about her tugged at the stubborn door of her heart. "She did?"

He nodded. "She wondered where you'd gone. And when Jamie told her you'd gone to your brother's, she wanted to know why we hadn't gone too."

"Oh." She had no reply, and her fuzzy brain could not form one. "How is your father?"

He paused at the change in topic then answered smoothly. "He is better, thank you. Jamie and Grace spent the better part of the afternoon with him. I was surprised at how easily Jamie opened up to him." He chuckled. "It might have had something to do with a promised pony."

She nearly groaned. "He asked your father for a pony?"

"No. I think Grace did. But once the ball started rolling, there was no stopping it."

She furrowed her brow. "Grace asked for a pony?"

"Grace already has a pony."

"And so does Jamie."

"But Bobo isn't here. And somewhere in the discussion that fact came out. So, Grace being Grace, she told her grandfather Jamie needed a pony too."

"Oh." His voice was soothing and she began to relax. "I'm glad he didn't feel abandoned. But he does love horses."

"I know. I will look around for a pony for him. I hope he doesn't pine too much for Bobo."

She should be annoyed Lion had obviously decided Jamie would stay at Edenvale, but at the moment she was just too tired. The sleeplessness of the night before caught up with her and, stifling a yawn, she leaned her head into the corner and closed her eyes. Within moments she was asleep.

Lion watched her relax into slumber, his thoughts reviewing their conversation. He hadn't meant to frighten her, but the thought of her denying Grace infuriated him. It was enough that she'd walked away from her when she was barely a fortnight old and hadn't bothered herself with Grace for five years. It was probably a good thing Grace was too young to understand the implications of a brother appearing she'd never known about. Amazingly, she and Jamie seemed to be just happy to have each other.

He turned to look out the small window, barely noticing the passing landscape.

His parents had exclaimed over how much Jamie had grown, and neither seemed to think it strange Emma refused to stay at Edenvale. He hadn't had much time to talk to his father, and his conversation with his mother hadn't revealed much, except she hadn't known that Emma was terrified of staying there. Unless her revelation that Charles was the only person able to get information out of Emma was relevant, he couldn't shake the thought that something else she'd said was important.

His mother hadn't known who Grace's father was, and he had no reason to believe his father might know. It was something he thought he didn't want to know. Charles had been much too forthcoming about Emma's amorous exploits, all the while complaining she'd rebuffed him and ignored his advice. Before yesterday, he'd not questioned Charles's statements. He'd only made a fool of himself whenever Charles mentioned Emma by arguing and, on more than one occasion, nearly starting a brawl. After yesterday, however, he questioned nearly everything his brother had ever said about her. It seemed disloyal somehow, but he couldn't forget Charles told him Emma had given Grace her name, but left her at Edenvale

118

because she didn't want to deprive his parents of both grandchildren. If Charles was to be believed, Grace wasn't their grandchild. So why not leave Jamie?

On the other hand, Emma admitted Grace had been too young to travel when she left. Perhaps, given the choice, she'd taken Jamie because she could.

Of course, none of this explained why Edenvale terrified Emma. Perhaps delving into that issue might explain everything else.

Chapter Eight

They stopped to change horses at Penrith. As Lion helped Emma out of the coach, he asked if she would prefer the opportunity to stretch her legs while the team was being tended. With the alternative being to wait in the inn's parlor, Emma gladly chose to walk a bit. Strolling away from the inn on Lion's arm, she breathed in the cool air and appreciated the sun on her face.

"I owe you another apology," she began. "I seem to be doing a lot of that of late."

He turned to look down at her, one dark eyebrow lifted in inquiry. There was no condemnation in his gaze, only curiosity. Perhaps her continued admissions that she might have been wrong surprised him. Perhaps not.

She hadn't slept very long in the coach. When she awakened, however, she'd kept her eyes closed as her mind reviewed their conversation regarding Grace. It had not been a good feeling, realizing how selfish she had been in abandoning Grace. Blaming a child for the actions of its father was the coward's way out. True, she knew Charles would not pay much attention to the child. After all, she was nothing more than a worthless girl. But that still did not condone her actions. Lion was right. What kind of mother abandons one child to lavish love on the other?

Lion was still watching her as if he expected her to bolt. She stopped and turned toward him, her hand lingering a moment on his sleeve before she dropped it to her side.

"I did not mean to imply Grace was not...our...daughter. Your mother made that quite clear to me before she was born...that...regardless of her real father's identity, the law would label her accordingly." She paused momentarily and looked away from his overwhelming presence, then forced herself to continue. He hated her already. What was one more reason? "The truth is that I...didn't...didn't...want her."

The stunned silence that met her comments did not give her any degree of comfort. She wished she could have been more forceful, more defiant. But it was hard to be defiant when you knew yourself to be in the wrong.

"Didn't...want...her?" Lion echoed.

"I didn't want to remember," she rushed on. "I still don't."

"What don't you want to remember?"

His voice was even, tightly controlled. A sure sign of anger. She almost wished for the angry Lion of earlier. The one who threatened banishment. That Lion she thought she understood. A lump rose in her throat, and she blinked back the gathering tears. She would not cry over the last five years. She'd managed to wall up her memories of the year before Grace was born. Yet Lion's appearance was slowly dismantling that wall brick by brick.

She turned away, raising her face to the sun and the cool breeze.

"If I answered that, I would have to remember."

"You can't run from the past forever, Emma."

She smiled despite the heaviness in her chest, knowing he could not see it. "I can try."

Even as she said it, she knew it for a lie. Perhaps once she was settled at Englevyn she could allow the wall to fall and take out the memories. Maybe then she could begin to construct an adequate explanation. In the meantime, her guilt would continue to demand her silence lest Lion not be willing to hear her out at all.

The sun was high in the sky by the time the chimneys of Englevyn came into view. Although still seated with her back to the horses, Emma recognized the landscape passing by the coach's window. The journey from Penrith hadn't been as tension-filled as the first part, yet they had still spoken little.

From the front, Englevyn appeared no larger than McKeown Manor. The deceptive facade concealed a large, comfortable home of three stories stretched out behind with small, terraced gardens concealed between wings that seemed to stretch to the horizon. Approaching the house from the fields on horseback revealed an extensive building of varying architectural styles tacked together by generations of Graysons that still managed to look stately.

As she'd learned the first time she'd stayed there with Jamie, the long corridors were a boon for an energetic toddler. She'd spent many hours in the wing housing the family portraits, thankful her parents had had their portraits painted before they all fell ill.

The front double doors opened as she alighted, revealing the butler, Riggs.

"Welcome back, my lady," he said as she entered the front hall.

"Thank you, Riggs. Is my brother at home?"

"No, my lady."

She was acutely conscious of Lion behind her as she asked, "When do you expect him?"

"I do not know. He has been in Carlisle for the last fortnight and left no specific date for his return."

"Then you must not have expected me," she guessed.

"On the contrary, my lady," he replied. "His lordship wrote just yesterday to tell us to expect you. A room has been made ready."

Thanking the butler again, she enquired about the possibility of a light meal.

"I will check with Cook."

Emma went upstairs to wash away the travel dust while Lion gave the coachman instructions. By the time she returned, he was waiting for her in the front salon, a glass of port in his hand.

"Sherry?" he asked, indicating the small sideboard.

"No, thank you. I asked Riggs to bring tea."

Silence fell between them, and she looked around the room to distract herself. Pale green wallpaper with climbing vines set the tone for the room. The cream upholstery on the chairs and sofas saved the room from being overwhelmed by the dark wood furniture and forest green rug. The sun shining through the window gave it a warmth it usually lacked, and she stepped into the golden pool on the carpet.

Lion moved to stand beside her. For a few moments longer, both stood silently staring out the window at the broad sweep of lawn. Lion broke the silence.

"Are you ever going to talk to me, or do you plan to continue this standoff for the rest of our lives?"

It was a valid question. One she knew needed an answer.

"I don't know," she replied. "Before you showed up at

Calderbrooke, I planned never to return." She turned to look up at him. "I had already decided if Jamie wanted to know more about his father's family, I would tell him once he was old enough to make the trip alone."

Astonishment crossed his features. "But that would have been years from now. My parents, certainly my father, might never have seen him again. Did that not occur to you?"

"Of course it did."

"And...?"

The door opened behind them and she turned to see Riggs enter with a tray.

"Cook says she'll have a simple luncheon ready for you shortly," the butler said as he set the tray down on a low table.

"Thank you," she replied, moving to seat herself before the tray. "And thank Cook for her efforts, please."

Lion followed after the door closed behind Riggs. He seated himself on a chair opposite her, watching her pour a cup of tea and add milk and a small amount of sugar to it. She settled back to sip her tea and watched him finish off his glass of port.

She was getting too accustomed to being stared at. Her hands barely shook under Lion's steady gaze, something that would not have happened even a week ago. Her heart, however, was still racing. Indignation was a powerful stimulant. She raised her chin and stared back at him.

"Are you going to answer my question?"

She took a sip of her tea while she mulled over a response. Telling him no would only frustrate him and possibly cause him to press harder. Telling him the truth would do the same, so why not?

"Truthfully, I didn't care whether your parents ever saw Jamie again. In fact, I was hoping they never would."

Taking another sip of tea, she closed her eyes against the storm brewing in his.

Even as she did so, she questioned why she was being deliberately cruel. When had she become so callous? So indifferent to the wishes and desires of others? Especially the family who had taken her in and raised her.

"You have become cold and unfeeling, Emma."

She opened her eyes and studied him. He sat forward, his elbows resting on the arms of the chair and hands clasped between. The young, handsome boy she'd married was gone. In his place was a man. A man with the sum of his experiences stamped all over him. The lean face and piercing eyes, the erect bearing, the aura of command.

This man would not have allowed his control to slip. He would not have seduced a fifteen-year-old and had to marry her. But if he had, he would not have run off to war and left her to fend for herself. He would not have expected his family to shoulder his responsibilities.

She finished her tea and set the delicate cup and saucer down on the tray. The door opened as she was about to speak, and she turned.

Riggs entered and announced luncheon was laid out in the breakfast parlor. Her relief at the timely interruption only lasted as long as the meal. After a meal of soup, an array of sliced meats and fish, potatoes, cheese, and topped off with a delicious fruit compote, Lion leaned back in his chair and twirled the crystal stemware in one hand.

The last of the dishes had been removed but Lion seemed in no hurry to move. Pity. She wanted him gone so she could pull herself together.

"Would you have Jamie write to me? I should like to know how he is getting on."

He nodded. "How long do you plan to stay?"

She looked away. The sunny yellow and crimson decor had no effect on her increasingly moody disposition.

"I don't know. I suppose that will depend on Jamie...and you."

"I see." He took a sip of his wine. "Do you plan to impose yourself on your brother indefinitely?"

"Not at all. Sooner or later I expect Thomas will marry. I will eventually return to McKeown Manor."

"And if I require your presence here?"

She hadn't considered that, having found her, Lion might refuse to allow her to return to the south. That would, indeed, make life difficult. Edenvale had too many memories for her to be comfortable there again. Yet, in all likelihood, there would come a time when she would have to face those memories. What would she do then?

The conversation had moved into uncomfortable territory. Lion knew by Emma's expression she hadn't considered that he might have some say in where she eventually lived. He wondered if she would disappear again once Jamie was off at school, especially if he forced her to live at Edenvale. After her hysterical flight yesterday, he doubted he could keep her there unless she was under lock and key, but he was curious as to what lengths she might go to in order to escape.

He and his parents had much to answer for, and he planned to get some answers upon his return. Despite that, he was aware that whatever had happened to her, he was primarily to blame. The naked truth was he should have never left her alone. Hindsight, however, would not solve the present problems. If they could talk it out, perhaps there was a chance, but her stubborn resistance had become almost insurmountable.

She had asked him once if he remembered the last words he said to her. If whatever he'd said was part of the reason she refused to return, he would have to think long and hard—and ask a lot of questions on his return to find out if anyone else knew what happened that April day. And if he could not uncover it, he would just have to ask her to tell him. The way he saw it, it was an important piece of the wall she'd built around herself. Perhaps even the cornerstone.

Draining his wineglass, he put it down and rose to his feet.

"It is time for me to head back. I want to be home before Jamie and Grace are put to bed."

She rose gracefully to her feet. Distant and cool. He often thought circumstances and situations made people what they are, and he wondered what had caused Emma to become the exact opposite of the bright, engaging, curious person she'd once been.

Crossing the entryway, he asked Riggs to send for his coach then entered the salon to wait. Emma followed.

"I will keep in touch and have Jamie write."

She came to his side as he spoke. "Thank you."

"I do not want to make life difficult for you, Emma," he said, "but someday we must come to terms with the fact that we are married. My parents will not be at Edenvale forever."

"I know." Her voice softened.

He turned toward her, his hand rising to touch her cheek. It was as soft as he remembered. Surprised she did not move away, he ran his thumb over her bottom lip. The green of her eyes darkened, yet she continued to stare up at him as if mesmerized. When her lips parted, he took it as an invitation and lowered his head.

127

He hesitated just shy of her mouth, expecting her to back away. Instead she lifted her face and touched her lips to his. He nearly groaned. For a long moment, he savored the smooth, mellow taste of her as his hand slid to the back of her neck and pulled her closer.

Delving deeper, he ran his tongue across her bottom lip then slipped it into the warm, moist cavern of her mouth. She tasted of fruit and wine. Sweet. Intoxicating.

Exploring gently, his tongue rubbed against hers in invitation. Her response nearly shattered his control as she kissed him back. Tentative at first, she grew bolder, inviting him to deepen the kiss as his arms went around her.

His confidence soared when she let out a low, breathless moan and melted against him. Gathering her closer, he was aware of her breasts pillowed against his chest, her thighs intimately pressed against his despite the layers of clothing.

If Riggs had entered the room minutes later, he might have found them doing more than kissing. As it was, Emma stared up at him in shocked disbelief when Riggs' discreet cough pulled them apart.

"I will be but a moment," he said to the butler before returning his attention to Emma. "You are not as indifferent as you would like me to think, Emma."

"Perhaps," she murmured. "But perhaps I wanted to discover something for myself."

"And what would that be?"

She stepped away from him. "That I was no longer the wide-eyed innocent girl who trusted you for protection."

"You may be right. But then again, I'm no longer that idealistic youth, blinded by a pretty face and lush body, who believed in the marriage vows we spoke."

She turned away, straightening her posture and lifting her head as she walked toward the hall. "It's time for you to leave. You don't want to keep the horses standing."

He crossed the room to her side as she reached the door. Putting his hand over hers, he looked down into cold, green eyes.

"Despite what you want me to think, you aren't as disinterested as you seem."

"I have become what your family made me. How you choose to interpret that is entirely up to you."

Once the coach was on its way, Lion tried to think over their conversation, but the memory of the kiss intruded each time. Her response stirred his blood, and only the thought of Emma's possible reaction to his return kept him from ordering the coach to turn around. He would bide his time and give her some space for a week or two while he did some investigating.

Something had gone terribly wrong that April day five years ago, and he intended to find out what it was. It might be the only way to save his marriage.

Emma spent much of the afternoon writing a letter to Sarah describing the journey north and Jamie's actions. Having told her friend very little about why she ran away, there was nothing to tell her about the flight from Edenvale. Not for the first time, Emma wished she had a female friend in whom she could confide.

While growing up at Edenvale, her old nurse, Mousey, had been her confidant. If not for Mousey, she might have done the unthinkable.

She wrote a short note to her brother informing him she'd

arrived safely and looked forward to his return.

Once those two things were done, she realized she had nothing to do. Looking around the small sitting room adjacent to her bedroom, she wondered what she was going to do with herself in the coming days. For the first time she considered her insistence on coming here. She hadn't wanted Jamie to feel he was being sent off with Lion alone. So she had accompanied them. Now that she was here, and Jamie was at Edenvale, she had no idea what to do.

If she had been at McKeown Manor, she would be preparing for the coming of winter. Ensuring there were adequate supplies, supervising the canning of fruits, drying herbs, and a myriad of other tasks that would require her attention. At Englevyn she could do the same, but only if her brother gave her the go ahead. Without his assent, she did not feel comfortable taking over the household. Besides, she knew from her stay before that his housekeeper was more than competent to handle such things. She thought wistfully of the list she'd left for her housekeeper, wishing she was there to assist.

Mary entered from the dressing room and asked if there was anything she needed. She glanced out the window, noting the bright sunshine.

"My cloak and bonnet for now," she replied. "I think I will take a short walk."

The air was frigid but not bitter as she let herself out into the first terrace garden. At this time of the year, the flowerbeds consisted of brown stalks surrounded by brown dirt mixed with decaying leaves. It would have been depressing if not for the mountains rising in the distance. Winter set in much earlier in the north, but there was a stark beauty about the gardens as she strolled past slumbering flowerbeds, setting her mind at ease.

Lion came to mind as she walked, the memory of his kiss sending warmth flowing through her limbs. It had only managed to prove to her what she long suspected. She was not immune to Lion. She might no longer be innocent and trusting, but impervious she was not. What she was, however, was afraid. And with that fear came a powerful motivation to keep herself out of Lion's reach. Something she now knew she could only do with marginal success. As long as Jamie needed them both, they would be occasionally in close company. How long could she resist telling Lion the truth about his brother?

As she descended the three steps from the first terrace to the second, it occurred to her that perhaps she was approaching the entire situation from the wrong direction.

What did it matter, after all, if she told Lion of Charles's perfidy? He could accuse her of making it up, or trying to blame someone unable to defend himself. There was no one to back her up besides her brother, and she hadn't told him the entire sordid story. There were some things she was too embarrassed to even tell her own brother.

Regardless, Lion couldn't think worse of her than he already did. Charles had already ensured Lion believed she was capable of the ultimate betrayal. And he had done so in her absence, when she could not have defended herself. What was the difference?

Perhaps telling Lion the truth would allow her to face the paralyzing fear that beset her each time she thought of entering Edenvale. The same overpowering panic that had driven her from the house yesterday.

By the time she reached the fourth, and last, terrace she was certain she could face Lion and tell him the truth of what happened five years ago. *And if he doesn't believe you?* She came to a sudden stop.

How much did it matter that he believe her? Telling herself it didn't matter was fine when she was alone and there was no possibility of it happening. Now it might. And she needed to be prepared for any reaction. Including the unwelcome possibility he wouldn't believe her.

Rounding the corner at the end of the gallery wing, a stiff, chilly breeze fluttered the ribbons of her bonnet and stung her nose. She stopped for a moment and raised her eyes to the vista before her.

The land continued to slope down to a lake, its surface rippling in the wind. Beyond the lake lay a woodland. She knew from her time here before that the small forest was home to myriad small animals and birds, and the lake was stocked with trout from the Eden river. The summer she'd spent at Englevyn with her brother and Jamie after Grace was born had been peaceful. If she hadn't completely healed from her emotional wounds, it wasn't for lack of a place to do so.

She would have remained with her brother if Charles had not come calling. Thomas had turned him away the first time he came and informed the household that she was never home to Viscount Lanyon. Unfortunately, Charles became a nuisance.

The overhead cry of a bird brought her out of her reverie. She would not think of Charles and how he ruined her life. She would think of the new beginning she had given Jamie, and decide how she would go about getting to know her daughter. She did not doubt Lion planned to bring Jamie and Grace with him the next time he came.

Turning her back on the lake and woods, she headed toward the stables then circled back through the kitchen garden and into the house again. She'd made her decision. The next time she had a chance to talk to Lion, she would tell him the entire story. If he didn't believe her...well, she'd decide what to do when that happened. Divorce was out of the question, and as his wife she had few choices.

Life was unbelievably unfair for women, she thought as she climbed the stairs to her room. With little she could do about it for the moment, she concentrated on what she could control.

For now, that would have to be enough.

Chapter Nine

By the time Thomas returned from Carlisle, Emma was heartily sick of her own company. She'd written two letters to Jamie, another one to Sarah, and one to her housekeeper at McKeown Manor. In addition, she'd spent time in the kitchen with the cook and housekeeper, both of whom knew her parents. She'd also spent hours in the gallery staring at the portraits of her parents and lost siblings.

Short walks out of doors helped, but with nowhere to go and little to do, it was an indicator of her situation that she seriously contemplated going back to Appleby. The same morning of her brother's return, she found herself wondering if she could face Edenvale again.

Preparing to partake of another lonely tea time, the fourth such since her arrival, she was in the library searching for another book to read when she heard approaching footsteps. The door opened and she turned, expecting to see the housekeeper with her tea tray.

"I see Lion still doesn't have the sense he was born with," her brother drawled.

"It's good to see you too, Thomas," she replied with a grin as he crossed the room in long strides to gather her into a warm hug. "I'm very glad you're here," she told him as he released her from the hug.

"I'm sorry I wasn't here to greet you," he said, "but I was certain you would be comfortable until I returned."

"I have been, thank you."

This time the knock on the door heralded the arrival of the housekeeper with the tea tray. After the woman left, Emma crossed to the chair before the table and prepared to pour.

"News travels fast," she commented, noting the two cups and many more small cakes and sandwiches than she could possibly eat.

He chuckled as he followed and lowered himself onto the sofa opposite.

For a short while there was only the click of china and rustle of movement as she poured them both cups of tea and each helped themselves to the array of delicacies. Once settled, however, Thomas glanced across at her and said, "I hope you know I didn't tell him where you were, even though I tried to persuade you to do so."

"I know," she replied. "Neither of us had any way of knowing McKeown Manor abutted the country seat of his closest friend."

He nodded, the dark red of his hair glinting in the firelight. "So, now what do you plan to do?"

She put down her cup and saucer. "I don't know." She bit into an almond biscuit, chewed and swallowed before she spoke again. "He thinks the very worst of me. I don't know if I can live with someone who believes such horrible lies about me. He might be glad to be rid of me."

As she spoke, the memory of his kiss returned, reminding her that neither of them was indifferent to the other. But physical attraction, she'd learned years before, was not the best basis for a relationship. And a purely physical response was deceptive.

135

"You think he plans to set you aside?"

Did she think that? She might have said yes the day after they met at Calderbrooke, but after the trip north, she wasn't so sure. Lion had been solicitous and gentle as they traveled. She'd even found herself speculating on whether he would accept her version of the events of five years ago. Her decision earlier in the week notwithstanding, she knew the largest barrier was one she'd erected herself. Unfortunately, she also wasn't certain how to tear it down.

"I don't think so."

"But you're not certain."

A vision of Lion's angry face in the coach when he issued the ultimatum regarding Grace flashed through her head. He had certainly been ruthless enough at that moment to do so.

"I...no, I don't know."

Thomas leaned forward and put down his cup and saucer before looking up at her again. "I doubt he'd want to drag his family's name through the mud in such a public fashion. I think it would be safe to say that, as he already has an heir, he might merely suggest the two of you live separate lives."

She'd considered the possibility. It hadn't given her any degree of comfort, however. She knew she would never take a lover, but how would she feel if Lion took a mistress? A sharp pain in the vicinity of her heart gave her her answer. She would hate it. She wished she knew why.

"You could return to McKeown Manor. It's yours, you know."

She looked up sharply, nearly spilling her tea. "Mine? How so?"

"It was left to you by Father."

She stared at him in speechless consternation.

"I said nothing to Lion," he assured her. "But you might recall I mentioned it to you once before."

"I remember you saying something about my dowry, and my being surprised there was one. But, no, I don't recall you specifically mentioning to me that you'd sent me to live in my own home."

He chuckled at her exasperation. "I suspect you were only concerned with whether I would tell anyone of your whereabouts."

She relaxed back into her chair. "I suppose I was."

They sat in companionable silence for a few moments. Emma ate another biscuit and poured herself another cup of tea as she mulled over their conversation.

"Is it part of my dowry, then?"

"No. It was part of our mother's dowry, but Father wanted to leave it to one of his daughters. He specifically left it to you with a small annuity, but left instructions for who it should go to next if you didn't survive. The solicitor said his will had only been written a month before he died."

"Oh." She was heartened to know she was not completely dependent on Lion.

"He also left you a generous dowry which would become yours if you were still unmarried at the age of thirty."

She fought to hide her dismay. She would have become an independent woman of means had Charles not made improper advances toward her when she was fifteen. Lion would not have made love to her because she would not have gone to his room for protection if Charles hadn't frightened her. If she closed her eyes, she could still recall Lion's face from that magical night. She had been so scared Charles would find her, she hadn't thought of anything except Lion would protect her. Look where it had gotten her.

The clock in the hallway chimed the half hour, drawing her out of her depressing thoughts.

"I hope I will see Jamie sometime while you are here. I'm certain he has grown significantly since I saw him last."

She smiled. "Of course he has. He is devoted to his pony, although he won't be seeing him much over the next few months. Poor Bobo."

"I'm certain Lion will be able to find him a new one whilst he's here."

Her smile faltered. "I suspect that is partially what I'm afraid of."

He watched her from under dark brows, concern creasing his features. Those deep emerald eyes were nothing if not sharp.

"You are worried that, having met his father, Jamie will no longer need you?"

Unable to voice the words, she nodded. Despite her bravado in telling Lion she had prepared herself for Jamie heading off to school in a year or so, she knew she was not ready to lose him to Lion and Edenvale.

Lion entered the library and found his father sitting behind the desk, looking over ledgers while his secretary waited. The earl had made a remarkable recovery in the last few days, and Lion's patience had worn clear through. After his talk with his mother had garnered no information, he'd been waiting until the doctor felt his father was up to being questioned. It had been an extremely long three days.

Lion's mother insisted it was Jamie's presence that speeded his father's recovery. Lion tended to think his father just needed the rest. Whichever it was, Lion was relieved that his father was well enough to be up and about. He had too many questions that needed answers.

The earl looked up now and noticed him. He gathered up some papers on the desk, slipped them into the ledger he'd been reading, handed it to the secretary, then dismissed the man with, "We'll finish this tomorrow."

Pouring himself a drink from the sidebar, Lion turned and raised the glass to his father, a question in his eyes.

"None for me, thank you," his father demurred.

Once settled in a chair across from his father's desk, Lion asked how he was feeling.

"Better," he admitted. "That quack, Sandstrom, says I need to rest more. That too much excitement will kill me." He snorted. "Staying in bed all day will kill me faster, I'd wager."

Lion chuckled. "Surely a little extra rest wouldn't hurt?"

"Bah! I'll get all the rest I need after I'm dead." After Lion's laughter died down, his father asked, "Did you get Emma settled in at Englevyn?"

The question sobered Lion instantly. "She seemed content when I left her." Had it only been three days since he left her? He'd thought about little except the kiss in the intervening time.

"Good." The earl seemed about to say something, but just sighed and shook his head, his shoulders drooping as he leaned back in his chair. "We failed her. Your mother and I had such high hopes for her, but in the end our family nearly destroyed her." The sadness in his voice was enough to remind Lion how much his father had doted on Emma.

Lion drained his glass and set it on the polished surface of the desk. "How?"

"The same way most things are destroyed. Neglect,

139

indifference, deliberate destruction. It happened so gradually that by the time anyone could have stopped it, the one person who could have refused to see the damage being wrought. Or didn't care."

Lion shifted uncomfortably in his chair. Was his father referring to him? If he'd been here, could he have stopped it? If she'd written him, could he have returned home fast enough to avert the disaster?

He'd already blamed himself numerous times for leaving her initially. Yet the letters he received those first two years had been lively and cheerful, containing long, running passages about Jamie's antics and progress. He remembered smiling and picturing his small son climbing onto chairs, stairs and getting into cupboards. First walking then running down the long corridors of Edenvale. He had missed much, but Emma reported each milestone in flowing description, allowing him to see everything. And if occasionally she asked if he was coming home soon, it did not worry him. His parents were taking good care of her and Jamie. If he hadn't wanted the adventure of the army, he might have been terribly homesick. Then, shortly after her birthday in August of 1814, the letters stopped.

Not long after her last letter, he'd received the first of many from Charles. Letters detailing Emma's exploits. He had not bothered responding to Charles, but had written to Emma directly, demanding an explanation of the activity Charles laid at her door. She never responded.

"I've often wondered," Lion ventured now, "if perhaps none of this would have happened had I not insisted on purchasing a commission."

"Certainly, it might not have happened as it did," was the response. "But obsession is a difficult thing to deflect. Perhaps if you had set up your own household."

Lion sat up straighter in his chair. "Obsession? What are you talking about?"

His father stared up at the beams crisscrossing the ceiling, a faraway look in his eyes. "We nearly lost her. We have certainly scarred her. There was no choice but to let her leave."

"Nearly lost her? Emma? When?"

The earl straightened in the chair, suddenly alert, and pinned Lion with his dark eyes. "Why, after you came, of course. I would not have even known you were here, but one of the stable lads was coming around the front to take your horse when he stopped because you hadn't dismounted." He frowned. "I don't want to repeat what I was told you said before you turned and galloped back toward town. Suffice it to say, it was not well done of you."

"I—" What could he say? Hadn't Emma told him that what he said to her that day was one of the reasons she refused to return? One of the reasons she wanted nothing to do with him?

"She was in a delicate condition, and after you left she went into a decline. She refused to eat, barely slept, and cried enough tears to fill a lake. Your mother was beside herself with worry for the health of the babe. I think if it hadn't been for Mousey, we would have lost her completely."

Lion had no response to the censure in his father's eyes. Hadn't his mother said nearly the same thing? It seemed he was doomed to disappoint everyone around him.

"Perhaps you could enlighten me as to what I said."

His father's mouth fell open then snapped shut. "Why? Don't you remember?"

"No, sir, I don't," he admitted. "All I remember about that day was seeing Emma standing on the steps. The next thing I remember was waking up with a very sore head at an inn somewhere between here and London."

The smile his father tried to lighten the atmosphere looked more like a grimace. "Went out and got drunk, eh?"

"I suppose so. And while that does not excuse what I said, I cannot apologize for something I don't remember. To hear you describe Emma's reaction, it must have been horrific."

"What do you remember of that day?"

Lion exhaled. "Unfortunately, not much. I had received a letter from Charles regarding Emma. So, when someone was needed to run some dispatches to London from Belgium, I volunteered." His father grimaced at the mention of Charles, but otherwise said nothing. "I didn't have much time. Even had I come inside, I could have only stayed a few hours before I would have had to head back. Emma knew I was coming somehow because she was standing on the steps when I rode into the courtyard. When I saw her, I-I didn't know what to think. I was in shock. Then I just turned and galloped away."

Had he not been watching him, Lion would have missed the flash of disappointment that came and went in his father's eyes as he tried not to squirm under his direct gaze. Not since he was Jamie's age had he felt so distinctly uncomfortable in his own skin.

His father let out a sigh. "That's it? That's all you remember? You don't remember calling her a whore?"

Shock rendered him speechless.

"Then, as you say, you turned and galloped off without giving her a chance to say a word." The earl's voice turned hard. "Not only did you appoint yourself judge, jury and executioner, you never even gave her a chance to speak."

The accusation was nothing more than he deserved. He was no longer surprised at his cold reception. Or her intention never to return, even though it meant Jamie might never know his grandparents. Or so many other things she'd said.

"But surely after Grace was born—"

His father shook his head. "It only got worse then. I was told she wouldn't even look at Grace. Refused to hold her. Wanted nothing to do with her. Your mother had to employ a wet nurse."

There was nothing he could say. Hadn't Emma told him she hadn't wanted Grace? Hadn't even known the child's name?

"The day she and Jamie left, I had the feeling I might never see them again."

Lion shook his head, trying to order his thoughts. "You knew when she left she never intended to return? Yet you let her go? Why?"

"I didn't know for certain she would disappear, but I think I knew she would not return willingly. Why should she?" His father looked at him. "I'll take that drink now. Whiskey, if you please?"

Lion refilled his own glass and brought his father one. His head was spinning, and he was positive the last thing he needed was a drink, but it was the only way to keep his hands occupied. He watched his father take a sip of the amber liquid.

"Why have you never told me any of this before?"

"You never asked. I assumed you had decided what to do. I had no idea you were still looking for her—not that I knew where her brother had sent her. I might have at least reminded you of what an ass you were that day. Perhaps then you might have understood why she disappeared at all."

Lion put down his glass to keep from crushing it. How did one refute the truth? "Who decided on Grace's name?"

"Your mother. She created it from Emma's names."

"I see." He picked up the glass and took a mouthful, studying the remaining golden liquid as he swallowed. The burn as it went down was only a momentary distraction. Did his father know the identity of Grace's father? After this past hour, he wasn't up for any more surprises, but maybe it was just something he needed to know in the end. To put it behind him.

"Charles was furious when he returned from London, but it was for the best."

Lion didn't care about his brother's whereabouts during the time. He was only interested in what his father knew regarding Emma and Jamie.

"His obsession," continued the earl, "was what caused the situation."

"Whose obsession?"

"Charles's. He was obsessed with Emma. Do you remember how angry he was when you and Emma wed? He'd come into this room only the day before and insisted the child Emma carried was his, and so he should be the one to marry her. When I reminded him you and Emma had both confessed that you were the father, he told me you were lying. It was obvious to me then that Charles had developed an unhealthy attachment to her." He finished off his drink and put the glass down on the desk. "Should I have said something? I don't know, but it seemed that as long as you were present, everything would work out."

Lion did not like where the conversation was headed. He already knew he was in the wrong and should never have left. Did he need to hear his father say it out loud?

"Even after you left, Emma and Jamie were fine. Your correspondence highlighted her days and, although she missed you, she was devoted to Jamie. Your mother and I were delighted she had become our daughter in truth."

There was nothing for Lion to do except listen. His father's reminiscences, while rambling, were providing him with information he had not known.

"As I look back, I realize everything changed when Charles came home to stay. His sporadic visits before hadn't been unusual. He occasionally played with Jamie and helped me with estate business in between visiting friends and making the rounds of local assemblies."

A terrible thought began in Lion's head. A question. Was it mere coincidence?

"When did Charles return?"

His father looked up as if suddenly realizing Lion was there. He blinked, then his brow furrowed. "Mmmm. The summer before Grace was born. End of June, I think."

June 1814. Lion felt as if he'd been kicked by his horse. The war was over then. The upstart emperor banished to Elba. Most of his friends were heading home, but he was still recovering from an injury and was too weak to travel. His closest friend, Major Max Dayton, stayed with him in Paris while he recuperated. They were preparing to return to England when a courier found them. Both had been requested to attend the Congress of Vienna as part of England's delegation.

Why hadn't he refused the request? Why hadn't he come home? The last five years could have been avoided. Of course, Max might have died from his wounds later at Waterloo if Lion hadn't been there to oversee his care, but Max hadn't. Because the two of them went to Vienna instead. And returned to Belgium in March of 1815 with Wellington.

Would events have played out differently if he hadn't volunteered to deliver some top secret dispatches, thereby bringing him back to London briefly in April? Speculation was a poor bedfellow when faced with the reality of subsequent events.

"She never told us, but I suspected. It wasn't until after his

145

death I knew for certain."

His father's voice drew him out of the cesspool of guilt into which he'd fallen.

"Told you what?" Despite the question, he was not certain he wanted to hear the answer. "Whose death?"

"Charles's death. Charles was Grace's father."

Chapter Ten

No! He wouldn't believe it. Emma didn't like Charles. In fact, he was the reason they'd had to marry in the first place. There must be some mistake. She would have never taken him into her bed.

The letters. Charles had written him letter after letter telling him of her rendezvous with others, but she'd pushed him away. Taunted him, even. According to Charles, Emma herself didn't know who among the many might be her child's father.

Lion had no idea he'd given voice to any of his thoughts until his father stopped him.

"Enough!" the earl roared, jumping to his feet to lean over the desk, the vein in his neck throbbing violently. "It's not surprising Emma refuses to return. Were I married to such a lackwit, I might have run off too." When Lion looked up at him in astonishment, he sank back into his chair and slumped in defeat. "What have I done to deserve such sons? One an out-and-out bounder, the other a fool."

The silence that descended was absolute. No sounds came through the windows or doors. Even the sound of the fire was suddenly hushed. Lion stared at his father, unable to find words. He had not seen his father this upset in years. Not even when Lion confessed to getting Emma with child. And then his father had not called him a fool.

"How do you know for certain?" he ventured.

His father's chest expanded as he took a deep breath that he let out in a long-suffering sigh. "After Charles's death, I pensioned off his valet. Before the man left, he came to me with a key he'd found while packing up Charles's possessions. He said he had no idea what it went to, but insisted Charles hadn't brought it with him from London. After he left, I gave it to Tuttle, who gave it to Mrs. Pennywhistle." He paused and finished off his whiskey. "She came to me later, in tears and nearly beside herself. She offered to leave her post because she had not known the key was missing from her ring of keys. I assured her she would not be turned off because a key went missing, and she would be housekeeper here for many more years."

Now that he was beginning to follow his father's thoughts, Lion knew where his father was going before he got there. All the same, he did not relish hearing it.

"The key was to Emma's bedchamber. She had mentioned to your mother that Charles had made himself free with her bedchamber at inappropriate times, and your mother merely told her to lock her door."

His father was right. He *was* a fool.

"Why did no one but Charles write to me regarding Emma?" It was a question he'd thought many times. It had seemed odd to him that not long after Emma's birthday the only letters he received from home came from Charles.

The earl looked at him in surprise. "I wrote to you regularly. So did Emma and your mother. But during a war one never knows if letters get lost, mislaid or if the person is just too busy to write back."

Lion shook his head. "During the last year and a half or so, the only person I received letters from was Charles. He kept me informed of what was happening at home. At one point he said you were ill, so I assumed you were too ill to write. He told me Emma was breeding, but refused to name the father. I wrote Emma asking for confirmation and an explanation, but received nothing in return."

"Charles, it seemed, said a great many things in his letters—many of which I would guess might not have been true."

A light knock on the door interrupted their conversation. His mother entered at his father's call.

"Ah, good. You are both here," she said as they rose to their feet. "It's time for tea. Grace and Jamie are restless."

Relieved, Lion waited for his father to come around the desk then the two of them walked toward the door.

"Does Mother know?"

"Know what?"

"About the key."

His father shook his head. "No. There was no reason to tell her. She was still grieving over losing Charles. I didn't think she could have handled learning of his deceit, especially as it concerned Emma."

"Thank you."

Dark eyes turned toward him assessingly. "Maybe you're not as big a fool as I thought. Now if you stop thinking everything Charles told you was the truth, there might be hope for you yet." Just before they reached the door, his father said, "I wish I had been more understanding at the time, but I had no idea the depths to which Charles had stooped. If it hadn't been for your mother, I might have sent Grace away."

"Do you think Mother knows?"

"I have no idea. We have never discussed it beyond the one

time she told me of Emma's complaint about Charles. After that, there seemed to be no more difficulties, so I let it go. I wanted to demand the name of Grace's father, but your mother insisted while she was breeding was not the time, especially as your mother was so concerned about her health."

Lion wondered if Emma would have confessed to his father what she refused to tell him. Of course, he hadn't asked her directly, so he really had no way of knowing whether she would truly refuse to tell him.

"But all that is old news for now. I wish I'd said something earlier. Maybe she would have felt she could return before now. I do miss her, you know."

Lion wasn't fooled. The best way back into his father's good graces would be to convince Emma to return to Edenvale.

Jamie did not seem his usual exuberant self during tea. Although he scarfed down his share of biscuits and cakes, there was something not quite right. Lion watched him until one of the maids, not the usual one assigned to the nursery, came to take him and Grace up to the nursery.

"What happened to Pearl?" he asked his mother after the children were gone.

"Sick," his mother answered. "I sent her home and told her to stay there until she was well."

"Has someone checked on her recently?"

"I asked Dr. Sandstrom to check on her. Why?"

"How long has she been sick?"

His mother studied him through soft, gray eyes. "Only a day or two, but Sandstrom reported one of her brothers and her youngest sister were sick last week when she had apparently visited them."

Lion frowned. "Did Jamie seem subdued to you?"

"No. But then again, he and Grace are so high-spirited. And sometimes he will settle down, so it is difficult to tell."

"Perhaps we ought to have the doctor come in and take a look at him. Emma would not forgive easily if Jamie came down with something."

The day had turned cool. A light snow fell from pewter clouds. Seated at a small table before the fire in her sitting room, Emma was answering a letter from Sarah when there was a knock on the door. Riggs entered at her call.

"This just arrived by messenger, my lady."

Emma took the proffered message and broke the seal. Lion's writing jumped off the page at her, and her blood ran cold. Scanning the rest of the missive, she looked up at the butler.

"Send word to the stables. I will need the coach readied for a journey. Where is his lordship?"

"In the library, I believe."

"Thank you." As the butler left, she rose on shaky legs and yanked on the bellpull to summon her maid. Then she resumed her seat to read the entire letter carefully.

After she set Mary to packing, she hurried down to the library.

Thomas was at his desk, looking over what appeared to be maps.

"Thomas, I have to leave," she said without preamble as she entered the room. "I just received a letter from Lion that Jamie is sick and the doctor suspects scarlet fever."

"Are you certain you should go, then? Scarlet fever is not to be trifled with." Thomas rose from his desk, his brow knit into worry lines. He met her halfway across the room.

"Yes. That's one of the reasons I have to go. I'm the best person to nurse Jamie because I've already had it. The doctor told Lion it is rare for someone who has survived it to contract it again, even if the person comes in contact with someone who has it."

"And maybe a sick little boy needs his mother?"

She smiled as best she could. "That too. I hope the weather doesn't hold us up too much. Lion's letter said he would have a coach with fresh horses waiting for me in Penrith."

"Would you like me to accompany you?"

She paused for a moment. It might be nice to have company along the way. Unfortunately, worry for Jamie would take any pleasure out of the journey.

"It's not necessary," she answered. "I suspect I won't be very good company with worrying about Jamie."

He grinned. "I don't expect you to keep me company, but I would try to keep you from worrying yourself thin."

She sighed and gave him a genuine smile. "I'm afraid that's just not possible, but I appreciate the thought. I'll have my maid along. I should be safe enough—unless you want to come."

"Not particularly. I was trying to be gallant." His lips quirked, and Emma thought someday some lucky woman would snag herself a true gem in her brother.

A half hour later, Emma hugged her brother and hurried down the steps to the waiting coach. Her maid already waited inside as Emma arranged her skirts on the plush seat. There was a basket on the seat beside the maid and hot bricks wrapped in flannel on the floor. She was thankful the snow wasn't heavier and it was melting as it touched the ground.

"Cook packed a basket," her maid said, "seeing as how we're leaving before luncheon."

Emma smiled in response but said nothing. Eating something would do her good, but right now eating was the last thing on her mind. She pulled Lion's letter out of her reticule and read it over again. He'd thought of everything, including apologizing for not coming to get her himself because he wanted to stay with Jamie until she arrived.

He'd also made arrangements for her to stay at the coaching inn in Appleby.

She closed her eyes and rested her head on the back of the seat. Just the thought of entering Edenvale again was already tying her stomach in knots. For Jamie, though, she would do it. She had to.

Reminding herself Charles was dead and could no longer do her harm helped calm her nerves. Perhaps if she limited herself to the nursery and nursing Jamie, she could blank out the rest of the house. The nursery was one of the few locations in the house Charles had not molested her in.

The trip seemed to take forever. At one point, Mary pressed her to eat one of the meat pies from the basket.

"Ye'll only work yourself into a tizzy, milady," she stated. "An' what for? For nothing. With that monster gone, there's no one to do you harm."

Mary was right, of course. "I know, but I still feel ill thinking about going back there."

The stop to change coaches in Penrith was short. Emma was thankful Lion seemed to have thought of everything in order to get her to Jamie as fast as possible. He'd even taken precautions against the weather for her comfort. They hadn't been needed, as the snow had stopped shortly before reaching Penrith, although the low-hanging clouds shielded the sun for the rest of the journey.

At his questioning, she'd told the coachman she'd decide once they reached Appleby whether she'd stop at the inn or go on to the house. There should have been no question but that she would go on to Edenvale, yet she couldn't quite say the words at the moment. By the time they reached Appleby, however, worry for Jamie had erased everything else from her thoughts, and she told the driver to carry on.

"Don't look, milady," Mary told her. "If you don't look, you can't see. Just get out and run inside and straight up to the nursery."

What sounded like an excellent idea in theory turned out not to be so in fact. Emma just couldn't bring herself to be so rude as to not speak to Tuttle as she entered the house. She lingered long enough to ask him to inform the earl and countess she'd arrived and hand him her cloak and bonnet before hurrying up the staircase. Memory kicked in and, before she had time to think about her surroundings, she was opening the nursery door and stepping inside the familiar outer room.

The nursery was made up of a large room and a medium-sized room, with a short hall off the medium-sized room which led to three smaller rooms. Hurrying through the large room, Emma entered the medium-sized room. The three smaller rooms off the short hall were used as bedrooms.

Poking her head in the first room, she found Grace curled up on a cot, fast asleep. She spared only a moment to take in the room decorated in greens and blues and note the rag doll clutched in the sleeping child's arms before moving to the next room. There she found Lion sitting in a chair before a bed on which Jamie lay. Both were asleep and she hurried over, checking Jamie for breathing and fever before turning her attention to Lion.

He couldn't be very comfortable in the straight-backed chair. With his chin resting on his chest, she couldn't see his face. She could see the growth of stubble on his face and deduced he must have been sitting with Jamie for much of the night before and into today. He was dressed for evening in simple black and white, but his cravat was untied and hung limply around his neck with the ends dangling down his chest.

Her heart squeezed at the sight. He looked so out of his element, yet entirely approachable. How would he react if she woke him?

A pitcher and small glass of water sat on a table near Jamie's cot, and a basin with water and cloths were on a small table near the door. If Jamie developed a fever he would need wiping down. Movement from the bed drew her eyes, and she turned to see Jamie looking at her. His face was splotchy and his eyes unfocused before they recognized her.

"Mama?" His voice was weak, and she went down on her knees to pull him into her arms.

"Yes, darling, it's me. How are you feeling?"

"Tired and hot. And my throat feels odd."

She stroked his hair, checking him again for a fever. Although warm, he didn't seem overly warm.

"Would you like a sip of water?" Picking up the glass, she helped him take a few sips.

"Are you going away again?" he asked once resting back on his pillow.

"No, sweetheart. I will be here. Rest now."

The small effort of conversation and sipping water seemed to have worn him out. His eyes drooped. "I'm glad," he murmured as he drifted back to sleep.

"So am I." The quiet voice came from behind her, but there

was no need to turn around to see who spoke. Only Lion's voice could make her pulse jump like a skittish colt.

Busying her hands smoothing the coverlet over Jamie, she took the time to allow her heartbeat to return to normal before she stood and faced him.

"You need rest," she blurted, then wished she could take it back. She didn't need him to know she noticed the lines around his mouth, or the pallor of his skin, or the red eyes that told her he hadn't slept much.

"You could say that." He stood and she stepped back. "I'm glad you made it so quickly. He was asking for you last night."

"Did he have a fever?"

Lion glanced down at their sleeping son and nodded. "Dr. Sandstrom said he wasn't certain Jamie had scarlet fever, but it was the most likely culprit. Pearl, the nursery maid, came down with it a few days ago. Her whole family has had it."

"Oh."

"Her youngest sister died; she was six, I think. They nearly lost one of her brothers as well."

"How awful. How is she now?"

"Sandstrom says she's on the mend, but will still be at least a week at home."

They were talking in low voices and moved to the door.

"Perhaps you should get some rest before you catch it as well."

"Worried, Emma?" His voice grew soft as his hand came up and touched her cheek.

She flinched away. "Not about you," she replied. "But once Jamie is well, I don't want to have to nurse you too."

His gray eyes softened as he looked down at her. "Would you?"

156

The storm clouds she often saw in his eyes were gone. Replaced by a sadness she couldn't interpret. "Would I what?"

"Nurse me should I fall ill?"

She drew herself up, staring at him for a long moment before turning to occupy the chair he'd just vacated. His soft laughter followed her as she closed her eyes against the devastating smile he'd given her before she turned away.

"Coward." There was just enough teasing in his voice to cause her not to retaliate, but she listened as his footsteps receded, and a distant door opened and closed.

She let out the breath she hadn't realized she was holding and opened her eyes to look down at her sleeping son. His skin was tinged with gray, but he continued to sleep peacefully, and she let out a sigh of relief.

It occurred to her that she should have asked Lion if the doctor was due to return today, but his smile and teasing air had disconcerted her. What was wrong with her that she couldn't be in his company for more than a few seconds before she wanted to be in his arms? He didn't trust her. Why couldn't she just forget him and move on? He would only hurt her again.

The last time he'd arrived home, when she was pregnant with Grace, was ingrained in her memory. The devastation had nearly driven her to do something she'd never considered herself weak enough to do. The thought that he had driven her so far as to consider suicide still made her insides twist painfully.

Lion entered his room and found his valet in a heated argument with Emma's maid.

"What's going on here?"

Two guilty faces turned at the sound of his voice.

"She says I have to make room for her ladyship's clothing," Liam complained.

Lion immediately saw the problem. The suite he occupied had two dressing rooms attached, but since there was only himself, his valet had turned the second dressing room into a room of his own instead of using the room set aside for him in the servant's quarters. Lion didn't like to displace him, but if Emma's maid felt comfortable unpacking her clothing here... The thought made Lion's blood run hot with anticipation.

For a long moment he had a vision of Emma in his bed, her fiery locks loose and spread over his pillows, her white skin flushed and dewed from their lovemaking. He nearly groaned at the erotic image and pulled himself back to the present.

"Sorry, old chap," he told the valet. "If my wife chooses to return here, you will have to move. For now, she is here, and there are no immediate plans for her to leave. So, off you go."

The maid smiled at him and curtsied. "Thank you, my lord."

"Don't thank me. I have yet to hear from your mistress that she intends to stay." He turned toward his dressing room. "I will ask her later."

As he entered the dressing room and began stripping off his evening clothes, tiredness pulled at him, but the memory of Emma kneeling at Jamie's bedside, the boy being held in her arms, occupied his thoughts. The way she'd reassured him of her presence and promised not to leave him, caused a small bit of hope to creep in. Perhaps she could be convinced to stay this time.

He would have to work out his apology. She deserved it. Moreso, she deserved to know he still loved her.

The talk with his father was still fresh in his mind. His

father told him Emma had continued to write letters to him. He had no doubt Emma never received any of the letters he wrote her in response to Charles's letters. In many ways it was a blessing. Those letters had been full of accusations and demands for an explanation of her behavior. In addition, at least one of the letters threatened separation and divorce. When he was still a second son, a divorce would have caused a scandal, but less of one than it would now. Now, however, divorce was out of the question.

He knew now he wanted her back. Would go to nearly any lengths to win her back. If she refused to live at Edenvale, they would live at one of the earldom's other properties. Perhaps move into the townhouse in Carlisle so she could be close to her brother. Or go back to McKeown Manor. He might enjoy living near his best friend. His only regret would be leaving his parents behind. There was also Grace to consider. He hoped Emma could see Grace for who she was and not as Charles's daughter, although he had no doubt prolonged exposure to the active and engaging five-year-old could melt the hardest of hearts.

Regardless of where she wanted to go, he would go with her. He'd lost her once. He would not do so again. Of course, all of this was contingent upon his being able to convince her he had been the biggest fool on earth in the first place and deserved a second chance.

When Liam entered the room to help him, he waved him away. "I can undress myself," he said. "I would prefer you find Carl and send him up to Jamie's room, then help out her ladyship's maid."

"Very well, my lord." Liam left him, and moments later Lion was crawling into his bed. It did not take him long to fall asleep, but he did so with the image seared against the back of his eyelids of Emma holding Jamie, assuring him she would not leave.

Dr. Sandstrom came to check on Jamie close to tea time. Emma was glad to see him. For the past hour, Jamie had been tossing and turning, and although he didn't feel any warmer, she worried his temperature might be rising. She'd sent Carl for a basin of fresh, cool water just in case.

"How's the patient today," the doctor greeted her jovially. She watched as he put down his black case and moved to Jamie's bedside.

"Restless, but he doesn't seem feverish."

He nodded. "Good. Fever is the worst part. If it doesn't come back, he's on the mend."

Jamie awoke as the doctor laid his hand across his forehead.

"He told me earlier his throat hurt. Should I have cook make up some broth for him?"

The doctor nodded. "A little tea with honey wouldn't hurt either." Then he turned his attention to Jamie.

Emma was heartened as the doctor asked Jamie questions about what hurt, how he felt, and so on. Dr. Sandstrom was new to the area. When she'd given birth to Jamie, another doctor had attended her. He'd died when Jamie was two, and there hadn't been an actual doctor in residence when she gave birth to Grace, so the local midwife had been summoned. As she observed this new doctor with Jamie, she was glad to note he wasn't gruff or condescending. He listened to Jamie's answers and responded accordingly. At one point he pushed the blanket back and raised Jamie's nightshirt, calling her over to show her the rash on Jamie's stomach and down into his groin.

"It's going to be a mite uncomfortable for a while," he said. "But it should go away in about a week. I'll give you something to put on it to help soothe it."

The doctor continued his examination, including looking into Jamie's throat. Emma noticed Jamie's tongue was bright red with a few white spots. She asked the doctor about it.

"That's why it's called scarlet fever," he told her. "The white spots are also on his throat. They can be quite painful, but will eventually disappear. Willowbark tea with honey will help."

Carl returned with the basin and some cloths, followed by a maid with an invitation to join the countess for tea. She used the doctor's presence as an excuse to refuse, but knew sooner or later she would have to face Lion's mother.

Once the doctor left, she sent Carl to find her maid then turned to Jamie.

"Well, young man, you have given your mama quite a scare," she said with a forced smile. "I hope the doctor is correct and you are on the mend."

Chapter Eleven

Lion awakened in time to dress for dinner. Liam had a bath prepared and clothing ready for him. As he shaved, he wondered aloud if Emma was still upstairs with Jamie. Liam didn't disappoint him.

"Your Lady mother invited her to tea, and again for dinner. Both invitations were declined."

Lion frowned as he cleaned the rest of the soap from his face. Did his mother feel slighted? If she did, he'd hear about it over dinner. Yet he understood. Jamie's welfare came first, even before her own. Which reminded him of something.

"Please see that Cook remembers to send up a dinner tray for her," he told Liam as he shrugged into his coat.

Both his parents were already in the drawing room when he arrived.

"Emma should have joined us," his mother complained as she handed him a glass of sherry.

"I'm sure she feels Jamie's welfare is more important for now." Lion didn't want to argue with his mother over Emma's choices. If she truly wanted to see Emma, she knew where the nursery was. He sipped at his drink.

"How long will she stay this time?" his father asked.

Forever, if he had any say in it. He couldn't just order

Emma to stay, he knew that, but he'd been pleased to find her maid arguing with Liam earlier.

"I'm not sure," he replied with a sigh. "At least until Jamie is well, I suspect. Beyond that is anyone's guess."

Tuttle announced dinner, and he followed his parents from the room, hoping the discussion regarding Emma was at an end.

An hour later, Lion climbed the stairs to the nursery. As he approached Jamie's room, he could hear Emma speaking with someone. He hesitated outside the door to Grace's room.

"I didn't think you'd want to stay in your old room, my lady," the voice he recognized as belonging to her maid, said. "So I put your things in his lordship's room. If you want me to move 'em to some other room, I will."

"I'd prefer not to share a room, but I'd also prefer not to cause talk among the servants." He heard her sigh. It was a mournful sound that tugged on his heart. "And you were correct. Putting me in my old room would only cause nightmares."

Silence fell. He heard the rustling of clothing, then the maid said, "How is the little one?"

"Apparently better than yesterday," Emma responded. "His throat is a bit sore, but he was able to put down some broth, and tea laced with honey and willowbark before he went back to sleep."

"'Tis good, then. And you, my lady?"

Lion was glad to hear the maid being so solicitous. If he couldn't get Emma to rest, surely her maid could.

"I've eaten. I'll be fine."

He wished he could see her face. Was she tired? Worried? She had to be. Had Dr. Sandstrom reassured her?

"Is there anything else you need?"

"No."

Lion didn't wait to hear more. He slipped into Grace's room, leaving the door ajar. Straightening a blanket that didn't need it, he smoothed an unruly curl back from her forehead and kissed her lightly. He heard the maid's footsteps receding as he stood and looked down at his daughter.

Regardless of what his father said about Grace's parentage, she was his. She'd always been his. Looking back over the time before Charles's death, Lion could not remember a single time when Charles paid the smallest bit of attention to Grace. Charles, more often than not, dismissed the child as a "worthless girl" and avoided her. It hadn't mattered then and it didn't matter now.

Leaving Grace's room and going down to Jamie's, he found Emma sitting in a rocking chair reading by the light from a brace of candles. The chair he'd occupied earlier sat near the end of Jamie's bed. She looked up, uncertainty in her expression.

"How is he doing?" he asked in a low voice as she put down the book and stood.

"Better."

His eyes roamed over her face, noting the signs of tiredness in the paleness of her complexion and the shadows under her eyes. The candlelight turned her hair into a fiery halo, picking out the reds and golds, and turning them into flame. He had to stop himself from reaching out to touch the softness he knew would be there.

The aroma of dinner lingered in the air, although the tray had been removed.

"If you would like to rest for a bit, I will sit with him," he said to cover the awkward silence that descended.

"I—uh—that would be fine." She seemed uncomfortable. "The doctor—"

"What did—"

In unison, they started and stopped. Silence again. She looked down, then off to the side. Tension radiated from her, and he wondered what had happened to cause her discomfort.

"The doctor said he seemed better. If the fever doesn't return, he's on the mend."

"Good." He wanted to reach out and touch her. To draw her into his arms and shield her from the nightmares she'd mentioned. How often did they plague her? Did she only have them at Edenvale? "You should get some rest." He stepped away from the door and farther into the room. "I will send for you if he needs you."

She looked back down at Jamie, then reached down and laid her hand against his forehead. "There's no fever. I think..."

Patience had never been one of his better qualities. "Emma." She was worried about Jamie. He understood that, but her hesitant manner was driving him crazy. What had happened to the woman who knew her own mind at Calderbrooke?

"You promise to send for me if he needs me?"

"Yes. Now go and get some rest," he moved closer, "before I decide to join you and you get no rest at all."

He was close enough to see the alarm in her eyes. "You wouldn't."

He held his tongue on a frustrated sigh. "I told you before, Emma. No, I wouldn't. Unlike Charles, I don't find pleasure in forcing anyone."

If he hadn't been so close, he would not have seen the small shiver that rippled through her small frame. She gave a

Denise Patrick

jerky nod of acknowledgment then hurried from the room. He stood where he was until he heard the distant sound of a door closing.

Did he know? What had Charles told him? He couldn't possibly know. If he did, he would hate her even more.

Sighing, she pushed open the door to his suite. Relief cascaded through her at the sight of Mary waiting for her.

"It's been a long day, my lady."

"That it has, Mary."

She was tired, but sleep was still a long time coming as she lay in the large bed. Lion's scent clung to the linens, and she buried her nose in the pillow. Would she ever exorcize him completely? Did she want to?

"Of course you want to, you ninny." She rolled over and sat up, wrapping her arms around her upraised knees. There were so many reasons not to trust him. So many reasons to cut him out of her heart altogether. "Such as?"

Such as causing her to talk to herself, for starters.

He hated her. Not the way he looked at her tonight. She'd definitely seen desire in his eyes tonight. The same desire that heated her insides all those years ago. So maybe he didn't hate her.

He didn't trust her. Had she given him any reasons to trust her? No, but she couldn't counter what Charles had told him about her. Of course, she didn't know exactly *what* Charles had told him. Maybe she should rectify that.

He thought she'd cuckolded him. Well, she had. But it hadn't been voluntarily. Was it the same if you had no choice? Was it worse that it had been with his brother?

166

What if she was ashamed of herself? Because she was. And it was very hard to expect someone else to forgive her if she couldn't forgive herself.

She closed her eyes as tears seeped from under the lids. That was the worst of all. The speculation that she might have been able to prevent what happened ate at her. Could she have fended Charles off if she'd acted differently toward him? Had she given him the impression she would welcome his advances?

Turning all the questions over in her head made it hurt. Time to think of something else and go to sleep. Tomorrow was another day. It had to be better than today.

She was counting on it.

Over the next three days, Lion and Emma took turns sitting at their son's bedside. The doctor had given both instructions to keep Jamie warm and quiet, feed him warm broth and tea, and put a salve the doctor left on the worst of the rash. It was exhausting and both merely fell into bed when the other one took over. Emma worried Lion would catch the dreaded disease, but she couldn't convince him to stay away. As a parent, she understood.

There were no further invitations to meals or tea, for which Emma was thankful. It was taking all her strength to cope with Jamie, Lion's constant presence and being inside the house. She had no idea if Lion had chosen his suite deliberately, but she was glad it was the first door she encountered when she came down to the second floor from the nursery. Not having to traverse the corridors of the house meant she didn't have to relive any terrible memories before entering their suite of rooms.

By the third evening, however, she'd convinced herself she might be able to stay in the house for an extended period of time. There were still certain rooms that just thinking about them turned her stomach, but there were other rooms where the memories weren't as disturbing.

She discovered, quite by accident, that there was no picture of Charles as an adult in the family gallery. Pictures of him as a child held no memories, but during the cold winter months, she knew the long, wide, second-floor gallery to be an ideal place for young children to run and play. And to be confronted by the face that had terrorized her for a year might be more than she could stand.

Lion wasn't certain what woke him from the light doze he'd fallen into. Before entering the army he'd been a very sound sleeper, but now the smallest of sounds often woke him. Jamie, thrashing around in his bed, was apparently the culprit this time.

The candle he'd brought with him was near to burning itself out. Lighting the candles on the brace left earlier provided him enough light to see the flush on Jamie's cheeks and note that he had thrown off his blankets.

Summoning Carl, he and the servant spent the next hour sponging Jamie down with cold water and spoonfeeding him willowbark tea. All the while they worked, he knew if Jamie took a turn for the worse and he didn't send for Emma, it would be one more setback in their already strained relationship.

As Jamie began to calm down and respond to their ministrations, he noticed again the scars he'd noted before. One in particular piqued his curiosity. A long, puckered scar along Jamie's upper left arm. It looked as if it was quite old and had been sewn together. Jamie must have been very young when the injury was received. What kind of mishap would create such a serious injury?

Questioning Carl was useless. The footman had not known Jamie before they arrived at McKeown Manor and had only been assigned to him earlier that year. The scar was already there when he started tending him.

As soon as Lion was satisfied they'd done all they could and Jamie seemed to be sleeping peacefully again, he dismissed Carl. Still kneeling beside his son's bed, Lion watched him carefully. His forehead was cooler to the touch now, his hair smoothed back and dark against the pillow.

He'd been such a fool. He'd thought himself a man as he marched off to war, leaving a wife and three-month-old son. His parents would care for them. And perhaps they had tried. But Emma and Jamie had been *his* responsibility, not theirs. If he'd been here, he wouldn't have missed the last eight years of his son's life. He wouldn't be looking down at an eight-year-old stranger and wondering who he was. He wouldn't be speculating about the origin of scars on his son's body. Nor would he be jealous when that child wanted his mother rather than the father he'd only met a month ago.

He turned at the sound of rustling behind him. Emma stood in the candlelight dressed in a blue flannel dressing gown that covered her from neck to toe. Her eyes were large in a pale face.

"What happened?" She moved forward to drop beside Jamie's bed.

Lion stood and caught her up against him. "He's fine," he said in a low voice. "His temperature went up a little, and Carl and I wiped him down until he was cool again. He's fine now." She seemed to sag against him. He wondered if Carl had sent her maid to get her.

She glanced over at the teapot and cup. "Did you give him

some of the tea?"

He smiled into her hair. "Yes. We got him to take almost an entire cup."

"What about...?"

"Emma. He's better now. I won't insult you by saying he's ready to go out and play, but he's better now." He was enjoying holding her against him. For the moment, it seemed the rancor between them was put aside, and he savored the feel of her softness against him. It was like a balm on an open wound. "Dr. Sandstrom said his fever would be up and down, remember? And this time it didn't take nearly as long to bring it down. I think he's on the mend." When she said nothing more, he asked, "What are you doing up? You should be sleeping."

She stiffened slightly before relaxing again.

"I woke up feeling Jamie needed me. I can't explain it, but I knew something had happened and I needed to be here."

He smiled into her hair. "A mother's sense?"

Her shoulders rose and fell as she took a deep breath. Reminding himself they were standing beside their son's sickbed was the only thing that suppressed his body's natural response to her breasts pillowed against his chest.

"Sit," he told her gently. "I'm sure you'd rather sit and watch him than return to bed."

"For a little while at least," she agreed, sinking into the rocking chair.

He took the chair at the foot of the bed, watching as she reached out and smoothed her hand across Jamie's forehead. The boy looked to be sleeping peacefully, and Lion fervently hoped his prediction about tonight's bout with fever being Jamie's last was true.

"You should get some rest now," she told him. "If you get a

few hours of sleep now, you'll feel much better in the morning."

He knew she was right, but somehow he did not want to leave her. For nearly the first time since he saw her at Calderbrook, they were not at daggers drawn. For the first time in years, they were in accord. Sitting at their son's bedside, it seemed as if the animosity that had peppered their relationship for the past month had vanished. Or perhaps it was just being held at bay. Even if he knew it hadn't, he wanted to stay here for the moment and pretend that all was right in their marriage, and in their world.

That she still loved him as he loved her.

He should say something, but he was reluctant to shatter the peace. Sitting in the chair watching her watch Jamie reminded him how keenly he'd missed her. And how much he needed her.

Now wasn't the time to voice those thoughts. She was focused on Jamie. As it should be. There would be time in the next few days.

He forced himself to his feet. "Perhaps I will take your advice and get some sleep," he said. "I will come and relieve you in a few hours. Then, at least, both of us will have had some rest."

Startled, she looked away from Jamie. For a moment, she merely stared at him in confusion. Then she smiled. It was as if the sun had risen in the room. "Good night, then. Sleep well." Then she turned back to Jamie.

"I will try," he replied and left the room.

Emma leaned back in the rocking chair and closed her eyes. Only the deep quiet of the house allowed her to hear his soft footfalls and the gentle closing of the outer door of the nursery. Oh lord, she was in trouble.

It had taken all her willpower not to melt into his arms. As it was, the deep breath had only filled her head with his scent. The same scent clinging to the bed linens.

Then he'd pushed her away. Telling her to sit. He'd been embarrassed by her clinging to him. Once seated, she hadn't been able to look at him. It had taken the last of her reserves to smile at him and let him go. A few moments more, and she might have flung herself at him and begged him to stay. To hold her. To comfort her. And promise her Jamie would get well.

In his arms, she could believe anything was possible.

Despite tonight's episode, she knew Jamie was on the mend. Perhaps tomorrow she would convince Lion to talk to her. Perhaps they could mend things. So far, she'd managed to stay in the house and not feel the same panic she'd felt before. Then again, she hadn't been in any of the rooms that figured prominently in her nightmarish past. What would happen when she entered the drawing room, or the music room? At least she needn't go back into her previous room.

She took a deep breath and let it out slowly, forcing herself to relax her shoulders and clear her mind. She would cross those bridges when she had to. For now, she would continue to concentrate on the reason she was there. She opened her eyes to look down at Jamie—and caught her breath. Standing beside the bed was Grace.

The little girl clutched a blanket in one hand and her rag doll in the other. Two red-gold braids hung down the back of her white flannel nightgown. Softly, so as not to frighten her, she said the child's name.

"Grace?"

The little girl turned to look at her. Her eyes were wide and dark, apprehension lurking in the green depths.

"You shouldn't be in here."

"I wanted to see if Jamie was better yet," the small voice replied.

Emma was at a loss. On the one hand, she didn't know Grace. Yet the mother in her responded to the woeful expression on her daughter's face.

She inhaled sharply as the words settled in her head. Her daughter. For a long moment, mother and daughter took each other's measure. Did she measure up? Would Grace push her away if she tried to offer comfort?

Shame washed over her for her actions five years ago. She'd blamed Lion for abandoning her and Jamie when she needed him most. At a time when she was vulnerable and feeling alone.

Grace would not have felt alone when she left her in the care of a wet nurse, Mousey and her grandmother, but she *had* abandoned her daughter. There was no way to sugarcoat the truth. Just as she accused Lion of abandoning her, Grace's eyes accused her of the same thing. It should not surprise her that Lion questioned how she lived with herself.

Impulsively, she held out her arms. "Come here, sweetheart," she invited softly, and was rewarded with Grace's immediate response. As she settled the small, warm body in her lap and covered her with the blanket, tears sprang to her eyes. "You know you should not be here because we don't want you to get sick too."

The little head nodded as she burrowed deeper against Emma's body and relaxed. Soft and warm, Grace smelled like soap and lemons. A yawn escaped and she settled again, hugging her doll against her chest.

Emma was reminded of Jamie at the same age. He hadn't the patience to allow her to hold him for long unless he was sick or tired, but she missed having him snuggle against her as Grace now did.

173

Why did I ever think I didn't want her?

Right now she couldn't think of a single reason for her to have turned her back on her own child. Even brief thoughts of Charles could not dilute the peace stealing over her as she rocked her daughter to sleep.

Lion stood in the doorway to Jamie's room, rooted to the floor. On the way down to his room, he'd remembered some of the candles had burned themselves out, and the others were getting low. It had taken him longer than he expected to find more candles and bring them back up to the nursery. So long, in fact, that he now stood transfixed at the sight of Emma and Grace asleep in the rocking chair.

Only one candle remained lit on the brace he'd brought up earlier, and he was glad he'd remembered. Treading softly, he replaced all the candles, lit one, and then left the room, stopping briefly to look back on the sight.

Mother and daughter slept peacefully. Emma's nighttime braid hung over one shoulder, blending with Grace's own braids and disappearing beneath the blanket. The lone candle cast a warm glow over their hair, causing the reds and golds to blend together, reminding him of a glorious sunset.

He wondered, briefly, why Emma hadn't sent Grace back to her own room. The last thing they needed was for Grace to come down with what Jamie had, but he didn't have the heart to wake either of them, and he wasn't certain he could remove Grace from Emma's arms without waking one or both of them.

For a long moment, he studied the two of them, noting the similarities beyond their hair. Both had a tendency to freckle and Grace, he knew, had more than her fair share of the little spots across the bridge of her nose and on her cheeks. Emma still had a few but they weren't as visible. The straight line of their noses and the oval shape of their faces were dear to him. And, in Grace, he often saw Emma at the same age. Irrepressible, fearless, happy, curious.

There was hope for them yet. If Emma accepted Grace, that was one less hurdle for them to overcome.

Chapter Twelve

Emma was awakened by the sound of Jamie's voice. Disorientation was followed by the realization she still held a sleeping Grace on her lap.

"Mama." Jamie rarely whispered, yet he was obviously trying not to waken Grace.

She smiled down at him and kept her voice low. "Are you feeling better this morning?"

He nodded. He was sitting up and looking at her with clear eyes, a bright smile on his face. "I'm hungry."

She shifted the warm bundle in her lap and managed to rise. "Let me go put Grace back in her bed, and then I'll send Carl up to help you wash up."

"Can I get up?"

She shook her head, hating to see the crestfallen face it caused. "Not until the doctor says so. But you can have a wash and change into a clean nightshirt. That will make you feel better."

Grace didn't stir as Emma carried her into her room. Emma kissed the baby-soft cheek before she placed her on the bed and covered her with the coverlet. Emotion welled in her heart and tears formed. Blinking rapidly to keep them from falling, she turned and left the room.

A short time later, after having sent for Carl and giving him strict instructions on what Jamie could and couldn't do, Emma re-entered Lion's suite. She was still tired, and now she also had aching muscles from holding Grace. She rolled her shoulders as she contemplated the source of their soreness. She knew she'd do it all over again.

Summoning Mary, she asked for a breakfast tray and ordered something more substantial than broth be sent up to Jamie before splashing water on her face. When Mary returned, Emma was curled up on a window seat in the sitting room. She'd pulled a small table near her and wrapped a blanket around her shoulders to keep out the chill.

Snow fell steadily as she stared at the gray-and-white world beyond the window. Even if Jamie was completely recovered, she wouldn't be able to head back to Englevyn any time soon. Her spirits didn't soar at the possibility of being trapped inside the house with Lion, but neither did the familiar panic come over her. Something akin to resignation settled around her instead. Perhaps they could talk their situation through.

"You sure you're warm enough, m'lady?"

Emma smiled at the maid. "I'm sure, Mary."

"I'll stir up the fire a bit more just in case."

"Thank you. Do you know if Cook sent some breakfast up to Jamie?"

"I didn't ask, but I'll check when I go back down." Mary tossed a scoop of coal on the fire then left.

Emma had finished her breakfast and poured herself a last cup of tea when a knock sounded on the door. Before she had a chance to call out, the door opened and Lion's mother entered. For a moment she was pleased to see the only mother figure she'd ever known, and then the countess closed the door and turned toward her. Her heart sank in her chest.

The countess was one of those women who seemed never to age. From the top of her beautifully coiffed mahogany hair to the tips of her indecently tiny feet, she looked like a young woman not many years out of the schoolroom. Unless, of course, she was looking at you with the same expression on her face she now turned on Emma. The scowl marred her normally unlined skin, and the hardness in her eyes leant certainty to the fact that this wasn't a call to welcome a daughter-in-law home.

Emma set down her cup and rose to her feet as the countess approached.

"Why are you here?" she demanded. "Why now? When it's too late." Her voice contained an edge of pain.

"Jamie needed me," was all Emma could think to say as she thought, too late for what?

"Where were you when he was looking for you? Was desperate to find you?"

Emma had no answer, but it didn't matter. The countess's eyes watered as she continued.

"He tore Carlisle apart looking for you. And your brother just threw him out. Said he had no right to see you." A tear slipped down the countess's porcelain cheek. "He was beside himself with worry for you. And you didn't care. Did you?" she accused.

"I...I'm sorry," Emma stammered, her heart pounding in her chest. "I...I didn't—"

"No! You didn't!" the countess hissed. "All the time you were hiding from him."

There seemed to be no stopping the countess.

"You were just teasing him. Playing games for your own perverted amusement. How could you do that to him? How could you cause him such pain?"

"I didn't mean to hurt anyone." The feeble attempt to derail the countess only incited her mother-in-law further.

"He cared for you. And you turned your back on him. Left him to go mad with worry and fear for you."

Emma backed away, pulling the blanket tighter around her as the countess moved closer. When her knees hit the edge of the seat, she fell back onto the cushion, looking up in alarm as Lion's mother leaned over her.

"You'll not be doing it again. You tortured my poor baby, but I won't let you do it again." The countess straightened and looked down at her with a mixture of pain, anger, grief and something else in her eyes. It was the something else Emma refused to name. Something dark and disturbed.

The silence crackled between them, and Emma felt as if she were suspended high above a yawning chasm, unable to defend herself completely yet unwilling to bear the entire responsibility for Lion's loss. Or his fruitless search. If he hadn't left them...

The countess suddenly turned in a swish of burgundy skirts and crossed the room to the door. As she opened it, she turned back. "I'll not let you drive Lion to his grave as you did Charles."

Stunned beyond speechless, Emma watched her leave and close the door none too gently behind her.

I'll not let you drive Lion to his grave as you did Charles.

All that had been about Charles? Not Lion? Charles!

Nausea attacked her stomach, and she finished off the last of her now cold tea to keep her breakfast down. Then she picked up a fringed pillow, drew her knees up and wrapped herself tightly in the blanket. Balancing the pillow on her knees, she rested her cheek on it as she watched the snow outside continue to fall.

She had no idea how long she sat there, her mind barely focused, yet oblivious to everything around her. Did Lion feel the same way? Did he blame her for his brother's death? Was that why Lion hated her? Did he think, like his mother, her absence had driven Charles to drink?

She wouldn't—couldn't—believe it. Charles hadn't been a drunk per se, but he drank enough on occasion to be beyond rational thought. That long ago night when she'd sought Lion's protection, Charles had been drunk. But it had not been a common occurrence. While she might not know what happened after she left, she doubted Charles drank more once she was gone. No, Charles hadn't turned to drink after she left. Of that she was fairly certain.

What he had most likely been was angry. Angry she'd escaped him. Thomas had only written her once regarding Charles looking for her, but she knew he'd gone to Englevyn looking for her more times than that. She also knew Thomas had thrown him out and given orders to deny him entrance.

None of that explained why the countess blamed her for Charles's death. Or did it?

She'd never told her parents-in-law who Grace's father was. Had Charles? Was that why they'd kept the infant? Admittedly, she'd given the child little thought when she left. She'd wanted no reminders of the terror Charles had put her through. Perhaps she'd known subconsciously Mousey would care for the infant. Or maybe her mother-in-law had become attached. Her memories of right after the birth were hazy at best, but she knew the countess had been delighted with the baby girl.

She could still hear the countess's disappointment-laden voice. *Regardless of the child's parentage, the law will consider it Lion's. So you'd best hope it's a girl.*

A sound behind her caused her heart to jump as she lifted her head and turned toward the door. Grace stood in the open door. She was still in her nightgown, clutching the same blanket and rag doll.

Before she could say anything, a young maid appeared.

"Miss Grace, you shouldn't be—oh!" Flustered, the maid curtseyed while trying to pick up the little girl. "I'm sorry, ma'am. I'll just..."

Grace took advantage of the situation, breaking away from the maid and running across the room. "Mama!"

Emma managed only to unwrap herself before Grace was climbing into her lap again. Suppressing laughter at Grace's antics, she looked up at the maid and smiled. "She's fine. What's your name?"

"Tammy, ma'am." The maid curtseyed again. "I'll take her back up to the nursery. Mrs. Pennywhistle will be sore put out with me if I don't keep her under watch."

"Has she had her breakfast yet?"

"No, ma'am, she just woke up. I was getting her clothes all ready when she snuck out."

She looked down at her little runaway. Grace had snuggled against her in much the same fashion as earlier this morning. It was a glorious feeling, but she couldn't encourage her to run away from the maid assigned to watch over her.

"Well, Miss Grace," she said. "What have we to say for ourselves?"

"Want Papa."

It was probably not unusual for Grace to come looking for Lion, which explained how the maid knew where to find her. "He's not here right now." Sitting up, she tilted the little face up to hers. "So why don't you go with Tammy and get dressed and eat some breakfast? Then, when you're finished, you can come back down here and see if your papa has come back." She softened the words with a kiss on Grace's forehead, then the tip of her nose.

Green eyes looked up at her, and she had the feeling she was looking at a miniature of herself. In that moment she found the most important reason to stay at Edenvale. Lion's mother was the only mother Emma had ever known, yet now she no longer looked upon Emma as a daughter. Now she considered Emma an instrument in her son's death. Would Emma truly want the woman who accused her earlier to raise her daughter? If Mousey had still been alive, Emma would be less concerned, but she wasn't.

Wrapping her arms around her daughter, she hugged her tightly then stood. Setting Grace on her feet, she said, "Now you be good for Tammy, and I'll be here waiting for you when you're all done."

Grace gave her a hug and a sloppy kiss then ran to Tammy.

"Thank you, ma'am. I'll bring her back in a bit."

"There's no hurry," she replied. Then they were gone, and she was alone with her new resolve.

Crossing to the bell, she rang for Mary. It was time to retake control of her children and her life.

Lion stood at the window of the inn looking out at the falling snow. It was so thick, he could not see to the other side of the road. He couldn't ride in this weather. He would have to wait it out—and hope it didn't take all day and night. Even this close to home, he didn't dare chance his horse or the package he was bringing home. All he could do was hope it would peter out soon.

He glanced behind him as the door opened. Sally entered with a tray of food. Another young woman trailed her with a mug of ale. Once she left, Sally set out the meal on the table.

"It's glad I am her ladyship is back now," she said cheerfully as he turned for one last look at the blizzard beyond the window. "'Twas dreadful right before the little one was born. I was afraid somethin' might happen to her. Even Mousey was worried."

Mousey? What did Emma's old nursemaid have to do with anything? Mrs. Moushell had been a widow when she was hired to tend Emma when she first arrived at Edenvale. Moushell had been a bit of a mouthful, so Emma had shortened it to Mousey. Even after Emma no longer needed a nursemaid, and a governess was hired for her, Mousey remained. When Jamie was born, Mousey was there to help Emma adjust.

"What happened to cause Mousey to be worried about her?"

"I dunno, but I heard Mousey tell her that killin' herself was the coward's way out, an' if'n she jumped, she would let him win."

"What?" He swung around so fast, Sally started. Two long strides brought him beside her. "What, I mean, who...who are you talking about?"

For the first time he could remember, Sally was speechless. She stared at him out of wide, horrified eyes, one hand covering her mouth. "I-I didn't mean to say anythin'," she stammered. "Weren't nobody s'posed to know. Cook always said someday I would say somethin' I wasn't s'posed to say."

"Know what?" he asked. "That someone tried to take their own life?"

She was trembling now, and her cheeks were painted red with embarrassment, but she nodded hesitantly.

"Who was it?" Lion's gut was tying itself in knots. A buzzing began in his ears. "And when was it?"

"'Twere a month or so afore Miss Grace was born, 'twas. I was cleanin' in the sittin' room off her ladyship's bedroom. I didn't see nothin' but I heard Mousey tellin' her how it was a sin to even think such a thing an' all."

Lion sank into a chair with a groan. How much lower could he sink? How many more ways could he be reminded of the emotional damage he'd caused Emma before he understood her disappearance and reluctance to return? His father was right. Their family had nearly destroyed her, yet now they expected her to return as if nothing had ever happened.

"Are you all right, m'lord?" Sally's worried voice interrupted his thoughts.

"Yes," he responded, "yes, I'm fine. I was just thinking." He straightened and turned to the repast she'd set out. "Thank you for the food. I may have to trouble you for a room if this doesn't lighten up soon."

She brightened at his words. "No trouble at all, milord. The one at the top of the stairs was just cleaned this mornin'."

The same room she'd given Emma.

Once she was gone, Lion helped himself from the dishes. He ate more out of habit than hunger, his thoughts on Emma. He didn't need to know anything more than "a month or so before Grace was born" to understand it had, in all likelihood, been the day he'd showed up unexpectedly, and was shocked into saying something so cruel it had nearly driven Emma to do the unthinkable.

He glanced up at the window as he finished the meal. The snow continued to fall, blanketing everything in a thick layer of white. He would not see his own bed this night. Perhaps it was for the best. His enforced seclusion would give him time to think.

By the time Sally came to clear the dishes, he'd come to a distinctly unpalatable conclusion. His father would understand better than his mother, but both would be disappointed.

Emma looked at herself critically in the mirror. The lavender trim of the purple wool gown matched the ribbons Mary threaded through her upswept hair. After a day of playing with Grace and arguing with Jamie, she'd considered ordering a tray in her room. Deciding to suddenly rejoin the family meant eating dinner with her in-laws, even if Lion wasn't there to provide support. After this morning's scene, she was not looking forward to it. Not only was she tired, but she was apprehensive. She and Grace had taken tea with the countess and nothing untoward was said, but there would only be the three of them at dinner, and she had no idea what the earl thought.

"Thank you, Mary," she said, rising from the stool. "You may go find your own dinner now."

Mary bobbed a curtsy and hurried off. Emma took a deep breath and one last look at herself in the mirror then followed.

Lion's father was delighted at her appearance.

"None of that, my dear," he said sternly when she went to curtsy. Instead he caught her up in a hug and bussed her soundly on the cheek.

She returned his hug and had to blink back the threatening tears. She didn't know what to think. The earl had always been warm and caring toward her, but this sudden, emotional welcome surprised her. He'd seemed so unapproachable to her as a child, although she'd never been afraid of him.

"Sherry, Emma?" the countess asked as she moved toward the decanters set on a table.

"Yes, thank you," she replied.

The countess's warm smile was confusing. As had been the case at tea, she showed no sign of the angry, grief-stricken woman who'd confronted her this morning.

"How is Jamie?" the earl asked.

"He's much better. Dr. Sandstrom didn't get here today, but if he doesn't make it tomorrow, I'll let Jamie up anyway. Today was pure torture for him—and not much fun for me either."

The earl chuckled as the countess handed him a glass. He took a sip of the amber liquid, then said, "I will be glad to see him again. He's a fine young man, Emma. You've done well."

Her heart warmed at the compliment. "Thank you."

The countess returned again and handed her a glass. "I don't know where Lion is," she said. "He left early this morning, but I expected him back by now."

"I'm sure he's somewhere safe and dry, Glenna," the earl said gently. "He's not prone to drink and wouldn't risk trying to get home in this storm."

Emma's heart skipped a beat at the veiled reference to Charles's death. She might be worried too, if she didn't trust Lion not to try something foolish. He might be in a hurry to get back—she hoped he was—but he would not risk his horse in such weather.

"I didn't know he'd left," she ventured now. "He was up very late with Jamie last night."

The earl finished his drink and set it down before putting an arm around each of them. "Now, ladies, there is no need to worry. I'm certain he will be back as soon as this storm blows itself out in a day or two."

Emma hoped he was right. When the butler announced dinner, she set her glass on the table as well, and turned to follow the earl and countess into the dining room.

Over dinner the conversation turned to the children.

"I think in the spring we will need to look for a governess for Grace," the countess said. "Otherwise she will feel left out once Lion finds a tutor for Jamie."

"It wouldn't hurt to have a governess for both," the earl countered. "Jamie will have plenty of male companionship when he goes off to school."

"I suppose it would depend upon the governess," Emma added. "Jamie has been tutored by the vicar in the past. Reverend Wight told me more than once Jamie might be ready for school well before other boys his own age." She hoped her comments wouldn't be seen as boasting, but she knew Jamie was a quick study. Even Lion had commented on it when he taught him to play chess.

"A governess like Miss Trimble would fit well with the two of them," the countess remarked.

Emma agreed. The years she'd spent learning French, Latin, history, mathematics and more under Miss Trimble's tutelage had given her a well-grounded outlook on life. Even though she'd also learned the more traditional "female" pursuits such as watercolors and music, they hadn't been her strong areas. No, she'd loved the allure of history and mathematics. And once she realized the benefits of being able to read history in the language it was originally written, she'd become entranced with languages. To have someone who could instill such a love for learning in her children would be ideal.

"Do we know whether Miss Trimble is still working and might be available?" she asked the countess.

A shake of her head was her answer. "I sent out inquiries earlier this year and learned she'd died two years ago." The countess took a sip of her wine then continued. "Very sad. She was such a wonderfully warm and intelligent young woman."

"I will work with them both until we find someone suitable." It would be a joy to read to and teach her children.

"So you plan to stay, then?" The earl's question reminded her she'd only made the decision for herself that morning.

She nodded. "I haven't had the chance to speak to Lion about it but, yes, I plan to stay." She looked down at the roast beef on her plate and spoke hesitantly. "I never thought to return when I left, but being back and becoming acquainted with Grace has shown me how wrong I was to leave. I don't know if I should expect Lion to ever forgive me—"

"Nonsense," the earl interrupted. "He, of all people, should understand what drove you to leave." He picked up his wine glass. "A toast to your homecoming. And we will speak no more of it."

She and the countess drank, but Emma wasn't certain about Lion's reaction. He might be glad she'd decided to stay, but he still might not trust her motives. Perhaps when he returned they could discuss it. She sighed. She was spending too much time thinking she and Lion could discuss their problems and not enough time trying to begin those discussions.

Looking back on the last five years, she realized how much she'd missed and how incomplete she'd been. It had been easy to block Lion from her thoughts. His last word to her had been so outrageous, so horrible, she'd had no trouble thinking herself a widow. After all, Lion might as well have been dead to her.

Since their reunion at Calderbrooke, she'd wondered more than once if he would have continued to look for her if Charles hadn't died. It was obvious to her he would have discovered her sooner or later as long as she stayed at McKeown Manor. Would he have forced her to return if Charles had still been alive? Would she have agreed to return if that had been the case? While those questions were all moot, they still left her wondering.

There was also the question of what she might eventually tell Jamie if he asked her about the last five years. It would depend upon how old Jamie was when he asked the question, but if it was tomorrow, she knew she'd be at a loss.

Chapter Thirteen

It was another four days before Lion returned to Edenvale. Four days during which Emma worried nearly constantly about where he was and what he was doing. The snowstorm blew itself out overnight, and the doctor made it to the house to pronounce Jamie fit to leave his bed. But Lion did not appear.

Emma dined with her in-laws, played with Jamie and Grace, and slowly reacclimated herself to the household, although there were still rooms she would not venture into.

She considered it a victory of sorts that she could sit in the drawing room without jumping every time someone entered the room. And as long as she avoided the window seat, she could stomach the long gallery—Jamie and Grace's favorite indoor playground. Yet there were still rooms she could not enter without experiencing mind-numbing terror, as she discovered the day Grace hid in her old bedroom during a game of hide-and-seek. She was thankful Jamie hadn't questioned her when she sent him in to check that particular room as the two of them searched.

Grace, she also discovered, loved to be read to almost as much as Jamie did. Of course, the two children's taste in material differed greatly. Grace wanted to hear fairy tales, while Jamie had become entranced by stories about knights and war. She was comforted by the fact that it was unlikely Jamie would go off to war if there were one in progress when he grew older. Heirs were rarely allowed to undertake such dangerous activities. Lion had only been allowed to purchase a commission because he wasn't the firstborn.

She didn't know if her near-apology of the first evening had satisfied the countess, but nothing more was said about Charles. However, the countess's behavior still confused her. There had been no other outbursts like the one in the sitting room, but there were times when she caught the woman watching her, a profound sadness in her eyes. If the countess refused to see the reality of Grace's parentage, perhaps Emma's return evoked memories she preferred not to revisit.

Emma sympathized with the countess in her loss, but she could not mourn Charles. He had made her life a living hell for nearly two years. More than that, he had caused Lion to hate and mistrust her, and then driven her from the only home she'd ever known. He'd also caused her to doubt—and sometimes hate—herself for how she'd handled the situation.

She knew when she left, Charles had no use for the daughter she'd borne. But she'd wanted no reminders of him. At least none she would have to confront on a daily basis. Now that she was back in her daughter's life, she was thankful for Lion's acceptance and championship of Grace.

"Check!" Jamie's voice interrupted her thoughts.

Startled, she looked down at the chessboard before her. "Oh dear." With Grace upstairs napping, the earl busy in his study, and the countess resting with a headache, Jamie had asked her to play chess with him. He was obviously missing Lion, to want to play with her. She was a terrible player.

She moved her king out of danger for the moment, but she could see it was just a matter of time. Maybe it was time to teach Jamie backgammon or draughts. She was better at those particular games.

A commotion in the front hall drew their attention, and moments later Lion entered the room. Jamie jumped up and ran to him.

"Papa! You're back."

Lion stopped long enough to hoist Jamie into his arms for a hug before setting him down. "You've grown since I've been gone," he said with a chuckle.

"I'm all well now." The pride in Jamie's voice made her smile.

"He's missed you," she said when Lion reached her. Soft gray eyes took her in from head to toe, and warmth unfurled deep in her belly.

"I missed him too," he replied, then he leaned toward her and in a whisper added, "but I missed you more."

"Papa, look." Jamie captured his attention again. "I put Mama in check."

Lion winked at her before turning back to look at the chessboard. "You did, did you?" He seated himself on the chair Jamie had occupied moments before, and pulled Jamie into his lap. Making a show of studying the board intently, he ventured, "It looks like you've got your mama's king cornered."

Jamie laughed. "I do, but I don't think Mama was paying very good attention. Abel's papa used to say if you don't pay attention, things will happen around you before you know it."

Emma laughed. "I'm beginning to think a certain little boy is just too good for his mama. You shall have to play with your papa from now on."

She watched the two of them discuss the position of the pieces on the board, her mind in a whirl. He'd missed her. Her! Not just Jamie and Grace. But her. Her heart beat a rapid tattoo in her chest at the thought. She didn't want to get her hopes up, but the look in his eyes made her want to shout with joy.

"What took you so long?" she heard Jamie ask.

"It took me longer than I expected to find what I went for. Then it snowed, and I couldn't get back as fast as I wanted." Lion's explanation made sense, but when he looked up at her there was something sad in the pewter depths. The joy of a few minutes ago diminished a little.

"What did you need to find?"

"Well, if your mama doesn't mind, how about if I show you?"

She smiled at Jamie's expectant look then rose to her feet. "I will just go and see if Grace is up yet. I'm sure she will want to see the surprise too."

Lion stood and said, "And we must tell your grandfather too. After all, he's the one who asked me to find it."

Jamie sprinted for the door, Emma and Lion following behind him. As they neared the entrance to the hall, she looked up at him inquiringly.

"If you'll remember," he said in a low voice, "my father agreed with Grace that Jamie needed a pony. So I was tasked with finding a suitable one."

"And did you?"

"I hope so."

She smiled. "I'm sure if you brought Jamie a pony, he will love it." As they reached the foot of the staircase, she said, "I'll go check on Grace and send down Jamie's coat and hat. We don't need him to catch a chill."

"Emma?"

She turned back, one foot on the bottom step. "I meant

what I said. I missed you." Then he bent and brushed his lips
against hers. "We will talk later."

Her feet took root, but she managed to nod in response
before he turned away, following the sound of Jamie's footsteps
down the hall.

Lion forced himself not to look back. Had he given himself
away? Had she guessed how much he wanted more? He sighed
and ran his hand through his hair as he turned the corner.

"I put Mama in check," Jamie was telling the earl. Lion's
father looked up and smiled.

"Glad you're back. Was beginning to worry. Did you find
what you went for?"

"I did, and fairly fast too. But then I took a detour to
Carlisle before I returned home."

The earl's eyebrows lifted toward his receding hairline.
"That's quite the detour."

"Papa has a surprise and says you should come and see it
too," Jamie interjected. "Do you want to come, Grandda?"

"That depends. Where are we going?"

Lion grinned as the earl stood.

"I don't know." Jamie suddenly looked at Lion in confusion,
and Lion chuckled, enjoying Jamie's enthusiasm. "Where is the
surprise, Papa?"

"It's in the stables. I didn't want to bring it into the house."

"Is it very big?"

The earl laughed out loud then, and Lion found himself
laughing along with him. Then he looked down into his son's
puzzled eyes.

"It was too big to carry into the house," he told Jamie as

they moved together to the door. Outside, Carl stood ready with Jamie's coat and hat. Once bundled up, Jamie hurried toward the back door and Lion let him go with—"Go ask Terence where the surprise is. We'll catch up with you."—and chuckled again as Jamie hurried out the door.

"You didn't let old Ned sell you a nag, did you?"

Lion was too happy for the moment to take offense. Watching Jamie's delight had warmed him thoroughly. Or perhaps it had been the brief touch of Emma's lips. Whatever it was, he barely felt the cool air as they exited the house in Jamie's wake.

"Of course not, but I did pay a little more for this one than Grace's. It's one of the larger cobs. After watching Jamie with his pony at Calderbrooke, I decided he could handle something a little larger."

"What does Emma think?"

Lion looked up at the bare trees as they passed through the edge of one of the gardens. The trees were cold, stark and devoid of greenery and he wondered if he was looking at his own future. He hoped not, but Emma deserved the choice.

"She hasn't seen it yet. She went up to see to Grace."

A congenial silence fell between them, their footfalls crunching against the partially frozen ground the only sound.

"For all that we've done wrong with Emma, bringing her together with Grace was the best for all concerned. Grace adores her."

Lion said nothing as they entered the stables. He could hear Jamie's voice echoing through the large building, exclaiming over the new pony.

The earl chuckled. "Let's hope there are a few good days ahead for him to get some riding in."

Lion agreed. The ponies were housed in the rear of the large building in slightly smaller stalls. Jamie stood before a stall, petting the new pony's nose. Beside him, Terence, was talking to him in a low voice while Jamie nodded.

"A right gentle 'un, he is, Master Jamie. An' jest lookin' fer a nice little boy." He handed Jamie an apple. "Likes his treats too."

Jamie giggled as he fed the pony his treat. Lion soaked in the sight, the sound, the smell. Not too long ago, he'd been angered at being deprived of times like this in Jamie's life. Now he was saddened. The soul searching he'd subjected himself to over the last two days told him letting Emma go was the right thing to do. It was unfortunate he couldn't convince his heart.

"Papa, Terence says this is my surprise. Is he really mine?" The awe in Jamie's voice reminded him that treats on this scale had been few over the last years. Emma had been frugal, unsure of her financial standing while living at McKeown Manor.

"Yes," he responded, "he is really yours. Grace has her own pony, and now so do you."

Jamie's expression lit up the entire stable. "Can I ride him now?"

Lion opened his mouth to say no, but hadn't the heart. "Perhaps a short time in the paddock wouldn't hurt. You could start getting used to each other." He nodded at Terence, who opened the stall door.

The earl studied the animal while Terence saddled him. "A fine specimen," he commented.

Lion agreed. Bobo was a smaller and lighter, dun-colored cob, but this new pony was a rich sable color with a dark brown mane and tail. It stood at least two hands higher than Jamie's previous pony.

"He's bigger than Bobo."

"You were doing such a fine job with Bobo, I thought you were ready for a little bigger one."

Jamie threw his arms around Lion's waist and hugged him. For a moment Lion was flustered. Grace was exuberant and demonstrative. She often hugged and kissed him. Lion had become used to giving both children hugs, especially in the evenings before bed, but this was the first time Jamie had ever initiated the contact. He reached down and returned the hug. "Thank you, Papa."

"All ready," Terence announced and Jamie turned away.

"So, what were you doing in Carlisle?" his father asked as they watched Jamie ride around the paddock.

"I gave orders to open the house. I want to take Emma and the children up for a bit of shopping."

"Excellent."

"I also stopped at Englevyn to speak to Thomas, but he wasn't there."

"We should invite him for Christmas," the earl said. "The poor boy has no one except Emma."

"We will drop in on him while we're in the area," Lion said. "I think he'd like to see Jamie and Grace."

Jamie's nose and cheeks were bright red by the time Lion called a halt to the riding and insisted they return to the house. Leaving Jamie with his grandfather in the study, Lion went in search of Emma. He found her in the sitting room of their suite.

"Grace is still sleeping, I noticed."

She smiled at him from her perch on the window seat. "She should be up soon, but this morning she and Jamie were running around so much they wore each other out. Jamie took a short nap after luncheon too." She leaned sideways, looking behind him. "Where's Jamie?"

"I left him with my father. They were talking horses. Jamie was explaining the differences between Bobo and his new pony and discussing names. It will be interesting to see what they come up with." He sat at the other end of the window seat, careful not to get too close. He wasn't certain of his control if he was within touching distance.

The weak rays of the setting sun burnished her hair, rendering her eyes dark as they watched him. For a few moments, silence filled the space as he took in her smooth cheeks and soft, kissable lips. His body stirred. What he wouldn't do for the chance to pull her into his arms and kiss her and... He sighed. That was not the reason he'd searched her out.

"Would you like to take a trip up to Carlisle? I thought we could take Jamie and Grace, spend some time shopping, and maybe even look in on Thomas." He stopped himself before he started rambling. When had he ever been so nervous? And with Emma of all people.

He'd thought this through many times over the last two days. If Emma wanted to live away from Edenvale, he would open up the townhouse in Carlisle. It was close enough he would still be able to see her and the children, and he hoped she might prefer it to Essex. There was the added benefit of her brother not being far away.

"I, uh, suppose so." She looked down at her hands in her lap. "I don't think there is anything I need, especially, but Jamie...and Grace—"

"Perhaps we can look for something for them for Christmas. Grace already has too many dolls, so I'm out of ideas. And I don't know what Jamie likes."

"How long will we be gone?" Her fingers worried the blue

twill covering her lap, pleating and unpleating the material in nervous movements.

"It depends on how long it takes to accomplish what we want," he hedged.

She raised her eyes to his. "When do you want to go?"

"I thought perhaps day after tomorrow, weather permitting. Is that acceptable?"

She nodded. "That should be fi—"

The door opened and Grace slipped in.

"Mama?" She hesitated a moment before she recognized Lion. "Papa!" A sunny smile lit her face, and she flew across the room to him.

Lion and his father regaled her with Jamie's reaction to his new pony over dinner. The countess sent her regrets and conveyed her happiness with Lion's return. Emma did not miss her, as she was still trying to determine exactly what the countess knew. Yet with Charles gone, Lion home, and she planning to stay, Emma wondered if it truly mattered now. Someday, she decided, she might ask. For now, it might dredge up old memories and a past that couldn't be changed.

After dinner, the earl dismissed himself to go check on the countess. With no particular reason to stay downstairs, Emma and Lion went up to the nursery. Grace was fast asleep, but Jamie was still wide awake.

"You ought to be tired after such an exciting afternoon," Emma told him as she tucked the thick comforter around him.

"I can't think of a good name."

"Ah." Lion expressed his sympathy over the predicament. "Then perhaps we shall wait a few days before bestowing a

199

name. That will give us time to think of an appropriate one."

Hugs, kisses and "good nights" were exchanged, and then she and Lion left. "It may still take him some time to get to sleep," she laughed. "Today ended up being quite an exciting one."

As they headed down the stairs and toward their suite, Lion looked over at her. "I rode out to Englevyn while I was in Carlisle, but Thomas wasn't in. I was hoping to take Jamie and Grace to see him while we are in the city."

"I haven't heard from him since I came here," she said. "But perhaps he has gone to Carlisle again. That's where he was when I originally arrived at Englevyn."

He opened the door to their room. Once inside, she stared at the bed, at a loss for words. She and Lion hadn't shared a bed in more than six years and now...well, now she was nervous.

"I will sleep somewhere else, if you would prefer."

Lion's voice startled her and she spun around. He was leaning back against the closed door watching her.

"I...uh...I don't think that will be necessary." She glanced at the bed again. It was very large. Surely they could both inhabit it. "I mean...it's...that is...the bed is large—"

"Emma." Amusement tinged his voice and he moved to her, taking her in his arms. The eyes that looked down at her were filled with tenderness and something else she dared not put a name to. "I don't want to make you feel uncomfortable."

"You haven't...you aren't." She took a deep breath, and his scent filled her head. She could feel the blush creeping up her neck and into her face.

He bent closer. "Are you sure?"

She wanted to close her eyes, but couldn't. The soft color of his eyes reminded her of the clouds before a storm, but there was no storm in his eyes. Only a mesmerizing gentleness that invited her in. Lifting herself up on her toes, she slid her arms around his neck and pulled him down to her.

Never in her life had she been so brazen, but right now she knew if he didn't kiss her she'd go mad. And since he seemed more interested in assuaging her sensibilities, it was time for her to show him what she wanted.

Later she might wonder why she hadn't spontaneously combusted when his lips touched hers. Instantly overwhelmed by the heat flowing through her, she lost any advantage gained by her boldness as Lion effortlessly took control.

Warm. Soft. Inviting. Lion's surprise lasted only moments before he tightened his arms and pressed her closer. And when she opened her mouth and lured him in, he was lost. He had not forgotten the kiss they'd shared at Englevyn. Despite her coldness afterwards, he'd wanted more. Now, in their bedroom, he planned to drink his fill.

His hands slid up her back, molding her curves to his solid frame. She fit perfectly against him. Like two halves of a whole. Tilting his head, he slanted his mouth over hers to delve deeper and slid his hand into her carefully arranged curls, scattering pins as the heavy tresses spilled down her back. A small shiver went through her, and a sigh escaped when he raised his head.

He caught a momentary glimpse of brilliant green eyes before dark lashes swept down to rest on pale cheeks. He kissed her brow then the tip of her nose, before resting his forehead against hers.

"Emma," he whispered hoarsely, "if you don't stop me now, we will definitely end up in bed together. And we won't be sleeping—at least not soon." He didn't want her to stop him. His control hung by a slim thread, but if he didn't give her the choice, whatever happened tonight would lie heavily on his conscience tomorrow.

Of their own accord, his nimble fingers dispensed with the buttons marching down her slim back. With her arms still locked around his neck, there was no chance the gown would fall, but it gaped tantalizingly in the front, teasing him with a hint of nipple beneath the thin chemise.

One hand sifted through red-gold spun silk, the other cupped a firm breast. Her breath hitched and she arched into the caress. "Don't stop," she breathed. "I—"

His lips traveled down the side of her face and cut off the words. No more were needed. Emma's hands feathered his hair as his tongue stroked hers in a deep, soul-drugging kiss that promised to last until one or the other needed more air. With her acquiescence, the thread of his control began to shred. It had been entirely too long.

His body protested its continued confinement as Emma's hands slid beneath his jacket, pushing it off his shoulders. What followed was a frenzy of movement, as they undressed each other in a flurry of kisses, caresses and rustling clothing. Then he scooped her in his arms and laid her on the turned-down bed.

A moment was all he needed to take in the desire in her emerald eyes, her full breasts with dark pink tips, trim waist, hips and long, shapely legs. He forced himself not to give in to his body's urging and fall on her like a starving man faced with his first glimpse of food. He wanted to love her as she deserved.

Joining her on the bed, he ran his hands over baby-soft skin, exploring the dips and valleys, curves and shadows, his lips seeking, tasting, savoring. A low moan tore from her as he took a rosy nipple into his mouth, and yet another when he moved to give the other nipple the same treatment.

He slid his body upward, moving his mouth back to hers as he settled between her thighs. Questing fingers found her hot, wet and ready, and his body refused to wait any longer. She was nearly as tight as she'd been their very first time. He encountered no resistance. Only a blissful sensation as he sank into her depths. A feeling like no other—a sense of coming home.

Instinct took over, their bodies falling into the ages-old rhythmic pattern. Her legs twined themselves around his hips then moved higher until he felt her feet in the small of his back. Slim, white arms wound themselves around his neck and pulled him in to a white-hot kiss, burning through the last shred of his sanity.

Lion surfaced through layers of lassitude, boneless and sated, with his arms still wrapped tightly around Emma. She didn't move when he reached down to pull the covers up over them. There was an unnatural stillness about her which prompted him to smooth a strand of hair back from her cheek and brush his lips across her forehead.

"Emma?" She moved slightly, but did not look at him. Had he hurt her? "Emma?"

She sniffed and his euphoric bubble burst. Pressing her onto her back, he stared down at her face. Her lashes were dark, spiky—and wet. Tears seeped from under closed lids into the hair at her temples.

"Emma?" *What have I done?* His mind raced through the evening, up to and through their lovemaking. Had he pushed her too hard? He hadn't coerced her, had he? She'd asked him not to stop, but had he been so overwhelmed by his need he hadn't truly listened?

Using a corner of the sheet, he wiped her face, but the tears continued to fall. Tentatively he put his arms around her, and was encouraged when she snuggled closer. She continued to weep quietly until she finally fell asleep, leaving him awake and confused.

What had he done?

Chapter Fourteen

Emma awoke in darkness. She was tucked in to Lion, her back against his chest. Her eyes were gritty, the skin of her cheeks tight. The pillow she rested upon was damp. Memories of the earlier events of the evening came flooding back, reminding her of the reason for her tears. She inched away and sat up, snatching up the sheet when it fell away from her naked torso. Beside her, Lion slept.

It had been so long since she'd awakened with another person that Lion's presence should have felt foreign. It didn't. Despite the embarrassment she felt at her earlier tears, Lion's presence was comforting.

She had some explaining to do, and it wasn't going to be easy. Truthfully, she wasn't certain how to explain her mortification or her tears. She took a deep breath and let it out as a long sigh. Would Lion even understand?

Rustling in the darkness and movement on the bed startled her, and she turned to look down at Lion. In the darkness, she could see the outline of his form but not the expression on his face, or in the eyes she sensed watching her.

"Did I hurt you?" His voice was quiet, disembodied in the darkness.

"No," she whispered.

"Then why the tears?" He sounded hurt. She wished she

could see his face because she didn't trust her own instincts.

Did he think she regretted their lovemaking? Did he? "I...I don't know if I can explain it." She sniffed as tears filled her eyes. She did not want to cry again.

His hand smoothed its way up her back then back down. Turning, she curled down into his arms and laid her head on his chest. The steady beat of his heart comforted her. His warmth and strength surrounded her. His seeming ready acceptance provided solace, but nothing could soothe the pain in her heart.

"I'm sorry," she whispered.

"Sorry for what?"

How did she explain she didn't trust herself? That she couldn't control her own responses. That no matter how much she hated Charles, she hadn't been able to convince him she did and that his touch was abhorrent. That somehow she had instead given Charles the impression she welcomed him. How did she tell Lion she hated herself...for the wanton she was.

Charles's voice rose up to taunt her. Telling her that, regardless of what she said, her body told him a different story. *Your body doesn't lie, Emma. You want me. Perhaps even more than I want you. And, someday you'll come willingly. But until then I'll just have to keep proving the words you throw at me are wrong.*

Wrong.

Wrong.

Wrong.

The words hammered at her, echoing through her head. She squeezed her eyes shut. She would not cry again. Charles was dead. He was gone. He could only continue to torment her if she let him.

"I don't know. I...just...am."

Lion was quiet for a long time. She was finally relaxing, having chased Charles's hateful words from her mind. Then Lion's chest rose and fell as he took a deep breath and let it out.

"I'm sorry too."

She lifted her head to look up in the direction of his voice.

"For what?"

"For everything. For being selfish. For leaving you and Jamie alone. For not understanding. For not listening. But most of all"—his hand stroked her hair—"for believing everything Charles told me."

"Why?"

"Because the truth was obviously a foreign concept for him. I should have realized...remembered...that he didn't like to lose. And when we married, he somehow equated it with having lost." He was quiet for a moment, then continued. "Regardless, I never thought he would go to such lengths to destroy what he couldn't have."

"How do you know it was Charles?"

"I'm ashamed to say I didn't. It wasn't until my father told me he was Grace's father, that I—"

She sat up abruptly. "Your father knew...?"

"Knew what?"

"That-that Charles had..." She couldn't finish her sentence. She did not want to say out loud that Charles had come to her bed. To voice it made it sound as if she'd welcomed him when just the opposite had been the case. And to think her father-in-law knew. The very thought made her nauseous.

"He didn't figure it out until after Charles's death."

Her stomach calmed a little. "How?"

"His valet found the key to your bedchamber among Charles's things and gave it to my father."

The chill in the room drove her back under the covers, seeking his warmth. She'd wondered if the countess had said something to the earl. After all, she'd told the countess Charles was making improper advances—for whatever good it might have done.

"But even my father doesn't know the lengths Charles went to."

"And you do?"

"I think so."

She was almost afraid to ask. "What lengths?"

"Do you remember the last letter you received from me?"

She wrinkled her nose—not that he could see it. "Sometime in August, just before my birthday. I remember because it was not long after that...that..." She couldn't finish.

"Charles began to force himself on you." She nodded. "Would you like to know the last letter I received from you?" She didn't respond, knowing he would answer the question anyway. "It was also just before your birthday."

"But I wrote—"

"I know. Or, rather, I think I know."

"Know what?"

"That you wrote to me more often." He tucked the covers tighter around her, pulling them up to her neck. "Once I began to realize you very likely hadn't received any of my letters, it was easy to assume I also hadn't received letters you'd written. So I did some digging. Jack Nydegger, who was postmaster at that time, retired shortly after Charles's death. I tracked him to his daughter's home in Carlisle." His demeanor changed, and his voice was hard when he said, "If he'd still been postmaster, I'd have had him arrested and transported."

She lifted her head to look in the direction of this voice. "You mean he didn't deliver letters you'd written to me?"

"It was worse. Charles paid him to withhold all letters and deliver them to him. Not only did I not receive your letters, but none that my parents wrote me or that I wrote to my parents were delivered either." She rested her head again on his shoulder. "I confess I'm relieved you didn't read some of the letters I sent—they were full of demands and accusations based on letters I received from Charles. I cannot but think your letters might have been pleas for me to come home."

Emma listened to him in stunned silence. It had not occurred to her Charles would have intercepted her letters to Lion. And as for his to her—she'd assumed he was busy and couldn't respond.

"Am I right?" he asked.

"Initially, yes. But once I realized I was...increasing, there was little I could do about it, and I didn't want to continue to distress you with a situation you could do nothing about."

Lion stroked her back, his touch light but warm. "Ahh, Emma. You have no idea how much your silence distressed me. I did worry something had happened to you, or Jamie. Once, in desperation, I enclosed a letter to you in one I sent to Charles. Unfortunately, with your silence, I had only Charles to rely on for news from home, and I have since realized nothing he told me was true."

She digested this information. Charles had done much more than nearly strip her of her sanity. He had attempted to completely destroy not only their marriage, but each of them individually. Why? What would he have gained from doing so? Was that why he was, as the countess put it, desperate to find her? So he could continue to torture her?

"My father said Charles was obsessed, and his obsession was unhealthy. Perhaps it's what drove him," Lion mused. "I don't think we will ever know."

Which was just fine with her. She didn't want to know. She'd be content never to hear or speak his name again. All it brought were horrible memories and a sick feeling in her stomach.

She yawned.

"Tired?" he asked. "Go to sleep then," he said when she nodded. "Tomorrow is another day, and we will have two excited children on our hands."

The last thing she thought before sleep overtook her was she hadn't explained her earlier tears.

Lion was surprised to find his mother in the breakfast room the next morning. He'd left Emma still sleeping, huddled under warm covers in a chilly room.

"You're back," she said unnecessarily, a delicate china teacup halfway to her lips. He watched her take a sip then return the cup to its saucer near her plate, before he answered.

"I am indeed." He approached the sideboard and began to fill a plate. "Did Father not tell you?"

She waited for him to be seated and looked askance at the nearly overflowing plate. "You must have slept very well to have such a hearty appetite this morning."

He chuckled. "Not as well as I would have liked. Emma and I were up late talking."

The countess's eyebrows raised. "She said she would stay. I hope you made it clear to her she should stay put."

He shook his head as he chewed a bite of pickled salmon.

210

"Why not?"

"That is her decision to make," he replied. "I'm glad she may decide to stay, but if she left again, I would not stop her."

His mother said nothing, but continued to watch him as he ate. He suspected she feared if Emma left, this time she would take both children with her. She was probably correct.

The earl arrived moments later. Once seated, he looked at Lion. "When do you leave for Carlisle?"

"What's this?" the countess asked. "You are leaving again?"

He smiled at his mother. "I am taking Emma and the children to Carlisle. While there, I hope to take the children out to visit their uncle at Englevyn and persuade Emma to add to her wardrobe."

"Ahh." She returned his smile. "Perhaps I ought to accompany you. I could introduce Emma to my dressmaker."

"Leave the boy to manage his own affairs, Glenna."

Lion winced. It had been a long time since anyone called him a boy. It was, however, better than the fool his father labeled him in the not too distant past. Just.

"There is no need. I remember who you and Emma patronized before," he replied.

"How long do you stay?" she asked.

"A fortnight at least, perhaps longer."

His father chuckled. "Or until Jamie misses his new pony and begs you to return."

"He will be able to ride him today," Lion said. "But we leave tomorrow."

By the time Emma joined them, he had finished his breakfast and was merely sipping his coffee while conversing with his parents. Greetings were exchanged and Tuttle was sent for tea while she served herself from the sideboard.

The earl insisted she sit beside him, which put her across from Lion. He didn't mind. It meant he could watch her and remember how soft and inviting she'd been the night before. The teary episode he easily pushed to the back of his mind for the moment.

This morning, however, Emma was subdued. She didn't look pale or drawn, but he could tell she wasn't herself. It was possible the emotional free-for-all of last night was to blame, and she just hadn't slept well. He would hate to think he was the cause, but he didn't know what else might be.

His father said something to her and she laughed. The transformation was breathtaking. Her whole face lit up and her eyes sparkled like emeralds. The smile stayed in place as she replied, the color in her cheeks taking on a life of its own.

Lion finished his coffee, enjoying the conversation between Emma and his father regarding Jamie and Grace's antics over the days he'd been away. It was good to see her happy. For the first time since seeing her in the Calderbrooke drawing room, he saw traces of the Emma he'd grown up with—the Emma he'd fallen in love with—and his heart swelled.

Grace's parentage was no longer of any consequence. Nothing mattered except that Emma looked relaxed and lighthearted.

His mother chose that moment to rise from her chair and, smiling at the three of them, said, "I do wish Charles were here to see us all together again." Heedless of the sudden silence her words caused, she continued directly to Emma. "He would be especially pleased to see you and Jamie back with us. He did so dote on both of you."

Emma's face blanched, her entire body stiffened and she looked down at the empty plate in front of her.

"Glenna!" Outrage infused the earl's voice.

Lion hurried around the table to Emma's side, gathering her to him as she stood.

The countess had turned toward the door, oblivious to the consternation her comments caused. Now she turned back, confusion in her expression.

The surprise in his mother's eyes reminded Lion that his father had told him his mother knew nothing about the key and, as far as he knew, did not know the truth of Grace's parentage.

"Why are you yelling, my lord? Did I say something displeasing?"

Lion locked eyes with his father for a moment then turned and led Emma from the room. The countess looked at the two of them through puzzled eyes as they passed her. Behind him, he heard his father say, "Yes, but you do not understand why. Come and sit."

It was very likely the truth. He did not doubt his mother knew nothing of Charles's activities. Beyond telling Emma to lock her door the one time, she probably ignored any other possible clues, and since Emma said nothing further, the matter was simply forgotten. His mother's comment regarding Charles doting on Emma and Jamie made him question if his mother's version of doting might not have raised eyebrows in another household. Perhaps if she hadn't considered Charles perfect, she might have seen his doting was aberrant.

Once in the hall, Emma sagged against him for a moment then straightened.

"I'm sorry," he said. "My mother obviously has no real notion of what Charles was like."

"She hates me." Her voice was flat. "She holds me responsible for Charles's death."

They walked up the stairs, pausing briefly on the first floor.

213

"Why would she do that?"

"Because I disappeared. She told me he looked everywhere for me. She implied he was desperate to find me and, when he didn't, he didn't know what to do. She thinks he started drinking because of it."

They reached the top floor, pausing before the door to the nursery. He put his hands on her shoulders, forcing her to look up at him.

"Emma, you are not responsible for Charles's death. If anyone was, it would be me. I was the one who was with him that night. I was the one who tried to pick a fight. And I was the one who left him at the inn, even though I knew he was drunk." He cupped her cheek with his hand. "We need to stop allowing Charles to dictate our lives. He's gone and, I hate to say it, but the world is better off without him."

"I know," she whispered. "But your mother doesn't think so." He hated to hear the misery in her voice.

"Perhaps not, but my mother has not been completely rational since Charles's death, and I know my father has been worried about her. Regardless, he will see she doesn't speak to you of Charles again."

A loud crash from the other side of the door cut their conversation short. Emma whirled around and wrenched open the door. Inside they found Jamie and Grace sitting on the floor amid blocks and toy soldiers, laughing.

"Mama, look," Jamie called. "We made a castle and the soldiers were guarding it, but the giant was too big and knocked it all down."

Grace giggled from where she sat, surrounded by blocks. "The giant was very big and the soldiers were too little."

Both children were still in their night clothes, but Lion noted the remains of breakfast on a side table.

214

Pearl came hurrying from the children's rooms. "Are you all right, Master Jamie? Miss Grace? Oh." The sight of Emma and Lion standing in the doorway stopped her.

Lion chuckled. "It looks as if they are fine, Pearl."

The maid dropped them a curtsy. "I was just setting clothes out so they could get dressed. Carl will be up in a moment to help Master Jamie."

"Excellent," Emma said with a smile. "If you will return the breakfast dishes to the kitchen, I think we can manage to dress them without putting anything on backwards."

Forty-five minutes later Lion, Emma, Jamie and Grace left the house headed for the stables. Despite the chill in the air, the sky was a brilliant blue, the sun dazzling in its intensity. As he and Emma watched the children with their ponies, her laughter ringing out at their antics, he was not deluded into thinking she had forgotten the morning's events. If anything, she was probably dreading luncheon.

Yet he knew his mother well enough to know embarrassment would keep her in her rooms until they left tomorrow for Carlisle. It was probably for the best and would give her at least a fortnight to think about whatever his father had told her, perhaps longer.

Chapter Fifteen

It had been a long day, despite having traveled in easy stages. Jamie and Grace weren't used to being cooped up inside a carriage all day, even though they took frequent breaks along the way. They stopped at Penrith for luncheon then spent some time walking around the town. Neither Emma nor Lion would admit they hoped to tire the children out, but there were no complaints when Jamie and Grace nodded off shortly after resuming their trip.

They reached Englevyn in time for tea and spent some time with Thomas before finishing their journey. The house in Carlisle was small, but plenty large for the four of them and their small cadre of servants. The housekeeper, Mrs. McGrath, and her husband who doubled as the butler, welcomed them into the cozy home.

After a hearty but simple dinner of soup, roast beef, potatoes and vegetables, topped off with fruit tarts, Emma and Lion took Jamie and Grace up to bed. Emma reflected that she enjoyed having the children eat with them, rather than being banished to the nursery.

"If those two get any sleep tonight, I will be surprised," Lion said as they left them in the care of Pearl and Carl.

She laughed softly as they descended the stairs. The last two days had shown her what she'd missed out on when she disappeared with Jamie five years ago. Family. She might not have wanted Grace, or to be found by Lion, but now that she had both she did not want to lose either again.

A decanter of brandy and a pot of tea had been left for them in the pretty little parlor decorated in muted tones of green and gold. Emma tucked her feet under her as she contemplated the fire and sipped her tea. Lion sat across from her in a matching green velvet upholstered wingback chair, a snifter of brandy in his hand. Outside a horse went by pulling a wagon, the wheels rumbling over the cobblestones like distant thunder.

Quiet descended, broken only by the flames crackling as the fire reduced the coal to glowing embers. Peace spilled through her, and she relaxed in the comfortable atmosphere. She set her cup and saucer down on the tray next to her chair, watching as Lion stretched his legs toward the fire.

Warmth spiraled through her as her thoughts went back to two nights ago. She had, for the first time in many years, felt loved. Did Lion love her still? Had his newfound knowledge of Charles's treachery erased his suspicions? Two nights ago, and even yesterday morning, she would have said yes. But last night he'd sent her upstairs alone and stayed up with his father. She hadn't heard him come to bed, although she'd awakened briefly in the night and remembered the weight of his arm about her waist and his leg thrown over hers.

"I hope you will consider adding to your wardrobe while here," Lion said.

Startled, she looked over at him. "I don't need anything," she protested, more from habit than in truth, "except perhaps gloves and boots. I don't know how, but I have managed to lose at least one glove every winter."

In the light of the fire, she saw him smile. "Grace also needs new gloves and boots, but her needs are the result of a growing child. Should I also assume Jamie needs the same?"

She laughed. "Yes, but he needs them for both reasons. Until I tasked Carl with keeping track of him, he also lost at least one glove regularly."

"Then we shall see to that in the morning, but I insist you see Mrs. McTavish in the afternoon."

Emma smiled at the memory of the dressmaker the countess patronized. Mrs. McTavish and her daughters were exceptionally skilled. The countess was convinced they could compete easily with the London modistes. Nothing, it seemed, was too difficult for them to attempt. All the countess needed was a fashion plate, and they could duplicate it.

The dresses she'd left behind five years ago still hung in her wardrobe, Mary had told her, but those were dresses for a younger woman. She was no longer the age of a debutante, and she didn't want to dress like one. That time of her life seemed so long ago.

In Essex she'd spent very little on clothing except for Jamie. For herself, she'd stuck to sturdy dresses, preferring comfort over fashion. The one ball gown she owned had been given to her by Sarah. Yet she understood Lion's wish. She, too, wouldn't mind a few new dresses. Having made the decision to stay, she did not want to embarrass Lion or the countess. There were only a few families in the area to socialize with, but there would be parties and gatherings around Christmas.

"Very well," she conceded. "I will see Mrs. McTavish tomorrow afternoon and order a few dresses."

"More than a few, I hope," Lion said. "At least one or two evening gowns and a ball gown. Although I don't think Mother is planning a ball this year, I expect we will be invited to a number of entertainments."

Emma stared into the dwindling fire. She was looking

forward to being back at Edenvale for Christmas. Jamie would love being part of the festivities and taking part in the decorating and other activities. It would be a joy to experience it through his eyes.

Lion put down his now empty snifter and leaned back in his chair. The movement drew her eyes, and she rested her head against the side of her chair. The silence was reassuring, and she allowed her eyes to close as the warmth wrapped around her.

It suddenly occurred to her she was happy. Not the excited, high-energy euphoria she might have previously associated with being happy. At this moment, in this place, and with Lion beside her, she was conscious of a bone-deep contentment. It was as if she'd been reaching for this moment for her entire life, or waiting for her life to begin. Her lips curled upward, and joy such as she'd never known suffused her entire being as a silent prayer of thankfulness was sent winging skyward.

Moments later she was conscious of being carried, then laid on something soft. She lifted heavy lids and found Lion above her. He was smiling.

"You fell asleep," he said softly as he began removing her half boots.

"Oh." Lethargy kept her still and compliant as he undressed her and slipped her nightgown over her head. By the time he joined her, she was nearly asleep again. Turning into his arms, she whispered a thank you then drifted off.

By the end of the first week, most of what they had come to Carlisle for had been accomplished. Mrs. McTavish and her daughters had promised Emma a number of items by the end of the fortnight, with the rest to be sent as soon as it was finished.

If not for that, Emma would have suggested they leave. Then it snowed.

And her brother arrived on their doorstep.

Jamie and Grace were delighted to see their uncle, viewing him as another person they could coax into taking them out to play in the snow.

"Tell me again why children never seem to get cold?" she asked Lion as she watched, from the warmth of the parlor overlooking the small garden, Jamie and Grace frolicking in the snow with her brother.

He came up behind her, sliding his arms around her waist. "You were the one who insisted Jamie did not handle the cold well."

"He will need a hot bath once he comes inside. They both will. At least they will have expended some of their energy."

Lion was quiet for a while then said, "It is good to see them having such fun. Children need to be children as long as they can."

She leaned her head back against his chest and sighed. "Yes, and Thomas too. He needs a wife and family of his own. If Sarah wasn't already married, I might have introduced them."

He chuckled. "I think Max might have had something to say about that."

"I'm sure he would, but she's the only young woman I know."

"I extended an invitation to Edenvale for Christmas. I'm sure there will be invitations from the neighbors for any number of parties. I think the Darnells have two unmarried daughters of presentable age."

"Did he accept?"

"He said perhaps. He is headed to Scotland to conclude

some business, and then he will decide."

The porcelain clock on the mantel chimed the hour, and Emma turned to look up at him. "It's time for them to come in. They need to warm up before tea, and Thomas will appreciate the reprieve."

He smiled down at her before bending to steal a quick kiss. "And I suppose I'm to be the one to spoil all the fun?"

She lifted up on her toes and kissed him back. "I will go and see if Mrs. McGrath has the water heated," was all she said before heading toward the kitchen.

By the time she left the children in the care of Pearl and Carl, the men had made themselves comfortable in the small library. As she approached the door, she heard her name and stopped to listen. As she did so, she should have remembered people who eavesdrop rarely hear anything good.

"So, you're planning to leave her here?" Thomas asked.

"With the children," Lion replied. "I can't let her go back to McKeown Manor. It's too far away."

"And you think she will agree to this...arrangement?"

"There's no other choice. She can't live at Edenvale."

"Can't...or won't?" her brother asked. "Or perhaps it's you who doesn't want her there?"

She didn't wait to hear more. She turned and nearly ran down the hall toward the kitchen. Stopping short of entering the room, she leaned back against the wall and closed her eyes.

Lion didn't want her at Edenvale. Had he brought her to Carlisle to leave her? To ensure she didn't return to Essex? Why hadn't he said something? When would he have told her? After all they had discovered regarding Charles, did he still not trust her?

Pain in the vicinity of her heart caused her to catch her

breath. She'd trusted him. After the last week, she thought they'd finally put the past behind them and started anew. He'd been gentle and protective, warm and caring. Had he purposely lulled her into compliance?

Footsteps coming down the hall jolted her out of her misery. Wiping damp cheeks, she entered the kitchen to see about tea.

How she got through the rest of the evening, she had no idea. Somehow she interacted with Jamie and Grace, helped get them to bed, and even spent time with Lion and Thomas before excusing herself by pleading weariness. She was only aware of a deep hopelessness threatening to swallow her whole. An aching emptiness where her heart and soul should be.

Lion watched her go with a frown. She hadn't been herself since tea time. Had something happened? Was she sick? Or just tired as she'd said? He'd never been skilled at reading women, but he thought he knew Emma by now.

Of course, she'd never explained her tears of a week ago, and he couldn't bring himself to ask. She'd told him she couldn't explain, but he was concerned something he'd done had reminded her of Charles.

Sally's revelation in Appleby finally allowed him to realize Edenvale held too many hurtful memories for Emma to ever be comfortable there. Her actions when they first arrived no longer surprised or shocked him. He understood not only had he made it worse by trying to force her inside, but when he'd carried her in, taking her up to her old room had been the final straw. He could only speculate on the nightmares that room must hold for her.

Lingering over their brandy, Lion thought Thomas wanted to say more to him on the subject of Emma. When he finally broke the silence, however, it was not about Emma at all.

"I leave tomorrow for Edinburgh," he said. "I have business with my uncle that cannot wait. I hope to return in time to accept your invitation to spend Christmas with you at Edenvale." He stopped a moment then asked, "You do plan to have Emma and the children at Edenvale for Christmas?"

"I hope to, yes." He'd already made it clear to Thomas that wherever Emma ended up would be her decision, not his. He could only hope she would choose to bring the children back to Edenvale.

"Good." Thomas rose to his feet. "Then I will retire and not bother you in the morning before I go. The weather between here and Edinburgh is changeable at this time of the year, and I do not know how long it will take me to get there, complete my business, and return."

Lion got to his feet as well. As the two left the small parlor and climbed the stairs, he turned to his brother-in-law. "Safe travel, then. I will look forward to seeing you sometime next month."

They parted and Lion continued down the hall. He hesitated at the door to his and Emma's room, his confusion over her actions returning. Alternating between hope she was asleep already and hope she wasn't, he let himself in.

Near total darkness met him. The small amount of light given off by the banked fire and lone candle on the table beside the bed revealed little beyond murky shapes and shadows. He took his time undressing, watching the mound in the bed for some sign she was still awake. There was something about the atmosphere of the room that told him she was, yet he did not trust his intuition this time. It had failed him with Emma much too often.

He slid into the bed beside her and snuffed the candle. She

was unnaturally still beside him, a telltale sign. Rising up beside her, he pulled her to him.

"Emma."

Sniff.

His heart sank. Not again. "Emma. Talk to me. I don't know what has happened to make you unhappy, but I can do nothing about it if I don't know what it is."

He all but held his breath waiting for her to answer. He didn't want to push too hard, but he hated being shut out. Too many misunderstandings happened when they didn't talk to each other.

"Why?" she finally whispered. "Why can't I live at Edenvale?"

Stunned, he closed his eyes against the gloom. Why hadn't it occurred to him she might have overheard their conversation?

"I thought...that...we..." Her voice trailed off and silence descended again.

He sighed. "If you only knew how much I want you with me at Edenvale, but I won't force you." He tightened his arms. "I tried that once."

"But I came back." She sniffed again, but her voice was stronger.

"Because Jamie was sick. I understand you would do anything for him—even enter a house that terrified you. But, Emma—"

"I'm not afraid any longer." He started to speak, but she continued, "Lion, I want to stay, but if you don't want me—"

It was his turn to cut her off. "Not want you! Oh God, Emma, how could you ever think that?"

Emma wished she could see his face. Bewilderment came

through his voice loud and clear. Did he not understand? Hadn't she made it clear she wanted to stay at Edenvale—with him?

"But I—" How did she ask without revealing she'd eavesdropped?

He seemed to read her thoughts. "I have to assume you heard me talking to Thomas this afternoon, but you obviously did not hear the entire conversation."

His hand smoothed over her hair as he turned onto his back, taking her with him. Draped over him, her head resting on his shoulder, she melted against him.

"I love you, Emma." She raised her head to look at him, but could not make out his features. "Between us, Charles and I nearly destroyed you. Charles deliberately, and I out of ignorance and youth. The last thing I want to do is hurt you again, but there is so much I don't know."

Her tears, for instance. He didn't need to say it for her to understand.

This was her chance. To tell him everything. Would he understand?

"I'm afraid to touch you, to suggest activity, to even speak, sometimes, for fear of saying something that will bring back the memories. When we were younger, you would never have backed down from a challenge, or a suggestion you couldn't or shouldn't do something. But now...now I'm terrified of triggering another nightmare. I don't like treating you like a china doll."

She sat up, pulling her knees up to her chest and wrapping her arms around them. Squeezing her eyes shut, she forced herself to relive the terror. Just one more time, she told herself. Then she could let it go.

"The first time Charles approached me, I pushed him away. He laughed, and I thought that was the end of it. Then he started coming into my bedroom. Sometimes I would be in the middle of my toilette, or worse, in my bath. When I told your mother, she said I should lock my door." The brush of Lion's hand toying with her braid was comforting. "Then one day he told me if I locked my door again, I would regret it."

The lump in her throat threatened to choke her, but she swallowed it down as Lion asked, "And did you?"

She squeezed her eyes shut against the memory. "The next day Jamie fell and cut his arm." The hand holding her braid fisted, pulling it tightly before relaxing again.

He sat up suddenly and gathered her into his arms. "The scar on his upper left arm?"

She nodded. "The doctor was detained, and your mother had Mrs. Pennywhistle sew it together." She could still see Charles watching her as she held her screaming son. The intensity in his eyes and the evil smirk on his face told her he'd won. She would never refuse him again.

"When I said something to your mother again, she insisted it was an accident. After that, I said nothing more. I couldn't." Tears sprang to her eyes again. "I was terrified something would happen to Jamie. I couldn't be with him all the time, and no one saw anything wrong if Charles wanted to take him somewhere."

She was crying now, her tears soaking his nightshirt as the words spilled out of her of their own volition.

"I didn't encourage him. I could barely stand to be in the same room with him, but I didn't dare refuse him. When he came to my bed, I tried to be passive. I thought if I did nothing, he would go away and leave me alone, but I didn't know." Her voice lowered to a shameful whisper.

"What didn't you know?"

She squirmed in his arms, her entire body heating with

226

embarrassment. How did one explain?

"It's all right, Emma," he murmured. "It's over. He can never hurt you again unless you allow it. I promise never to speak of it again."

She sniffed and burrowed closer to his warmth. She needed to block out Charles's hateful voice as he described how her body responded to his touch.

"I didn't know—didn't understand that doing nothing only made him angry. That it became a challenge for him. That I made things worse because he only tried harder to wring a reaction from me. A reaction I could never give." She wanted to retreat to the deep, dark corner of her mind where she'd cowered as Charles tormented her body with his hands and mouth. Lion said nothing for a moment, and she hoped he wasn't disgusted with her.

"I'm sorry, Emma," he finally said in a broken whisper. "I know the words have little meaning so long after the fact, but I don't know what else to say."

She understood. Hadn't she told herself that with Charles gone, she had to move on? "When I realized I couldn't stop him, I would close my eyes and think of you." It was the only thing that kept her sane. The thought that Lion would come and save her. "I told myself you were coming home soon. You would make him stop."

He groaned, and she knew he was thinking of their conversation of a week ago. There was nothing to be done about Charles's actions. It was all in the past, but he *had* asked.

"Mousey and Mary were the only people who knew," she whispered. "I made them swear not to tell anyone else."

"I am especially thankful Mousey was there for you. I don't know what I would have done had I returned to discover you had taken your own life."

227

She gasped and her stomach clenched. How had he found out? Surely Mousey hadn't told him.

As if reading her thoughts, he said, "Mousey told me nothing before she died." He was silent for a moment then said, "Although I'm glad she did not break your confidence, this past month would have been very different had she'd said something to me other than merely urging me to find you."

"How...how did you...?"

"Find out? Purely by accident," he replied. He shifted her nearly onto his lap and pulled the coverlet tighter around them. The fire had burned down, and the room was cooling rapidly. "What happened, Emma? It *was* the day I returned, wasn't it? The day I rode in and back out without even dismounting?"

She began to shake. She opened her eyes to keep from remembering, but the darkness took her back anyway. She was frozen on the steps of Edenvale watching Lion approach. She was ecstatic to see him. Even the fact that she was nearly eight months pregnant with Charles's child couldn't overshadow her joy. She would explain and he would understand. He'd make certain Charles never touched her again.

Then he'd taken one look at her, and she'd seen revulsion and disgust in his eyes. Even before he spoke. And she realized Charles had been right again.

"Charles said you'd hate me. He said you wouldn't want me any longer. But I didn't believe him. I knew you'd understand if I told you what happened. And you would—"

Lion went completely still at her words, dragging in a harsh breath. His arms tightened spasmodically, cutting off her breath. She looked up where she knew his face should be and internally cursed the darkness. She wanted to know what he was thinking.

"I should have known Charles would be right again," she

finished in a near whisper, dropping her head against his chest again.

She sensed his hesitation before he asked, "What happened after I left?"

Indecision swamped her, yet she heard herself respond. She never thought she'd ever tell anyone how she'd stumbled back inside, her sight blurred by tears. How she'd dragged herself up the stairs to her room feeling dead inside. And how she'd climbed up on the window seat, opened the casement and, in a moment of weakness, nearly stepped over the sill.

"Mousey found me standing there. She'd already heard what happened and had run up the stairs to find me. She said you hadn't meant what you said, but I knew better. I knew you hated me."

"I don't hate you, Emma."

She knew he didn't hate her now. That was not the problem. "You did then."

"I suspect I thought I did," he admitted. "Charles had done a thorough job."

She understood that now—five years after it happened. But that nineteen-year-old hadn't known or understood. She'd been frightened, lonely and desperate.

"Yet none of it excuses the fact I didn't trust you. And for that I'm truly sorry." His hand came up and stroked her cheek. "I will make it up to you, love."

Even though the room was cold, Emma was warm and the warmth was making her sleepy. He was already making it up to her. His acceptance of her explanation had given her back the peace she hadn't realized she was missing. She yawned.

He kissed the top of her head and said, "Perhaps we should continue this conversation in the morning." She heard the smile in his voice.

"You might be right," she murmured as she tried to stifle another yawn. Contentment stole over her. Just as she had the first night they arrived in Carlisle, Emma found herself nodding off.

Lion sank down into the bed, taking her with him. He pulled the heavy quilt over them both and tucked her into his side. He was certain she'd fallen asleep, yet that blissful state eluded him. His mind was too busy going over their conversation.

From now on, he promised himself, he'd tell her what he was thinking. Charles had stolen her self-confidence. He would try his best to give it back.

Chapter Sixteen

"Do you ever wonder why Charles did what he did?"

Lion looked up from his plate of eggs and regarded Emma across the small table.

"I do," he replied. "I thought about it quite a bit once I realized what he'd done."

She took a bite of egg then picked up her teacup. "What did you come up with?"

He watched her take a sip of her tea as he marshaled his thoughts and formulated an answer.

"Charles didn't like to lose," he began.

"No one does," she interrupted, remembering he'd said the same thing at Edenvale.

"True, but Charles was obsessed with winning. That obsession is what I think drove him." He took a sip of his coffee. "If he couldn't have what he wanted, he would not allow anyone else to have it either."

"I see." She set her cup down and took a bite of toast. "I don't remember him being like that when I was a child."

Lion shook his head. "I'm not sure he was. Like you, I don't remember him being so obsessed, but even as a boy he hated to lose. Everything was competitive with him. Perhaps it had something to do with him being the heir, but he always felt he had to have first choice."

"I know I shouldn't feel sorry for him, but he's not here and I am, so I can afford to be generous."

Lion chuckled. "I should as well, but he had me so thoroughly convinced you were little more than a light-skirt that I find it hard to forgive him—or myself. He no longer needs my forgiveness, but I am having a difficult time forgiving myself."

She finished her toast, all the while watching him. The look in her eyes told him she forgave him, but that still didn't absolve him. Charles had stolen his trust. Trust in her and in their marriage.

"When we met at Max and Sarah's, I knew you didn't trust me."

Lion's bark of laughter might have been funny if it wasn't so derisive.

"Trust. Faith. Confidence. You have no idea how many times I told myself I trusted you. Charles had to be misconstruing something. Then I destroyed it all with one word spoken in shock." He laid aside his napkin.

"I understand now, I think."

He shook his head. She didn't understand. She had no way of knowing how Charles's words had eaten at him over the past five years. Of the poison those words had become, and how easily he'd succumbed to their deadly bite.

"Then tell me." Her lips turned upward, but her eyes watched him with empathy. "I think, after last night, the best we can do is get it all out on the table then let it go. If we don't speak of it now, it may fester like a wound and eventually destroy us anyway."

He sighed and sat back in his chair. "I never wanted to tell you this."

"I suspected as much," she said gently. "But there were things I never thought to tell you."

She was right. He knew she was, but it didn't make what he was about to tell her any easier. A sliver of dread lodged itself in his heart.

"You told me last night when Charles first approached you, you pushed him away." She nodded. He took a breath to steady his nerves. "That may be the only kernel of truth in all the letters I received from him, but he said so much more."

When she said nothing more, he continued.

"He never mentioned names, but he said you were cavorting with other men. He insisted you always rebuffed him, and when he tried to say something to you about your affairs you laughed at him."

"I see."

"Do you?" he asked, his voice soft. "Do you realize that what he told me meant I never even considered he might be Grace's father? That for years I have been tortured watching her grow up, wondering whether the footman who paid special attention to her, or the stablehand who saddled her pony, or the gardener who picked flowers for her was her father. That I suspected every man from Edenvale to Appleby? Every man except the true culprit?"

Her eyes widened and filled with unshed tears. "Oh, Lion. I had no idea. I thought Charles would have gloated—bragged even—about what he did. He certainly led me to believe he had." She dabbed at her eyes with her napkin. "It was one more reason for me to get away. I felt as if everyone knew. Until your mother spoke to me while you were gone, I thought she knew. Then she all but accused me of causing his death." She sighed and her shoulders sagged.

His heart hurt at the sadness in her voice. That he'd been a

233

partial cause of it filled him with remorse.

Sliding back his chair, he came around to hers and pulled her up and into his arms. She was warm and soft, and he never wanted to let her go.

"After all my family has done to you, tell me again why you want to stay?"

She raised her head. "You should know why by now," she whispered. "Because I love you—and Jamie needs his father."

His heart swelled at her words. After last night, he was afraid she would never say those words to him again. He'd laid himself and his feelings bare. And, though he'd not expected a similar response, he'd still been disappointed when she hadn't reciprocated.

He bent his head close to hers. "My family and I do not deserve you, you know."

"Perhaps." She smiled. "But it has taken us five years to realize what we have missed—and what we have deprived our children of. I once thought I hated you, but now I know I hated myself because of what happened."

He raised his hand to stroke her cheek. It was soft and warm, just like his heart.

"I never hated you," he said, brushing his lips against her forehead. "But I didn't want to let myself love you again. The hurt of betrayal was lodged too deep." He kissed her nose. "Then I saw you again and I knew I had to have you back. That nothing mattered beyond having you home, seeing you smile and laugh again."

She raised her face to his, her lips parted. He needed no invitation to take her mouth in a long kiss. Their tongues tangled as their bodies pressed intimately against each other. She tasted of sweet tea and passion.

He raised his head a fraction and spoke against her lips. "I will never let you out of my sight again, my love." He cut off the sigh that escaped in his hurry to taste her all over again.

The years fell away, and they were young lovers all over again with their hopes and dreams laid out before them.

Giggles reached his ears, and he raised his head to find Jamie and Grace standing in the doorway.

"Was there a reason we didn't close and lock the door?" he asked Emma.

She looked up at him with the sun in her eyes, dispelling the clouds beyond the dining room windows. "It doesn't matter," she replied with a grin. "We will tonight."

Then she turned and held out her arms. As he watched their children run to her, the last of the ice melted inside. It might be cold outside, but here, in the cozy warmth, watching his wife and children, Lion knew he'd never be cold again.

As for Emma, he hoped the scars of the past were healed. He would devote the rest of his life to never causing another one.

About the Author

A well-traveled military brat, Denise developed a love of history and other cultures during her formative years. Reading came as naturally as breathing and once hooked on romances, she determined to write one herself. Historicals are her first love when it comes to romances, especially the Regency period.

She and her husband live in the western U.S. and have two grown children. They love to travel and their current destination of choice is Germany. Someday she hopes to make it to England to see firsthand the places she has studied and writes about.

Visit Denise on the Web at: www.denisepatrickauthor.com

Or on her blog at: http://denisesden.blogspot.com

Double trouble—with a twist.

The Scarred Heir
© *2012 Denise Patrick*

Two months. Just two more months and Sarah Standish will be twenty-one and free to come out of hiding. Not long ago she was on the brink of marrying the man of her dreams—until she discovered his complicity with her uncle's plan to gain control of her missing father's substantial fortune.

A wounded man appears at the inn where she lives under an assumed name, and she's shocked to discover it's her would-be groom. He seems to have no memory of her, yet her traitorous heart remembers.

Max Dayton awakens from a fevered dream to find a vengeful angel hovering over him. When he realizes she's mistaken him for his twin brother, his protective instincts kick in. There must be some reason his brother assumed Max's identity...and some connection to this dazzling beauty and the father she insists is not dead.

In a quest to untangle the twisted trail of lies that threw them together, Sarah and Max journey to London, where the mystery grows darker and deeper. And the fragile beginnings of love are threatened by a secret someone would kill to keep.

Warning: Contains a war hero, runaway bride, jealous twin, greedy uncle, and a good reason to check names before proceeding. At least the dog knows who is who.

Available now in ebook and print from Samhain Publishing.

Her heart longs for justice, but her body clamors for sin.

The Runaway Countess
© *2012 Leigh LaValle*

Once the darling of high society, Mazie Chetwyn knows firsthand how quickly the rich and powerful turn their backs on the less fortunate. Orphaned, penniless and determined to defy their ruthless whims, she joins forces with a local highwayman who steals from the rich to give to the poor.

Then the pawn broker snitches, and Mazie is captured by the Lord Lieutenant of Nottinghamshire. A man who is far too handsome, far too observant...and surely as corrupt as his father once was.

Sensible, rule-driven Trent Carthwick, twelfth Earl of Radford, is certain the threat of the gallows will prompt the villagers' beloved *Angel of Kindness* to reveal the highwayman's identity. But his bewitching captive volunteers nothing—except a sultry, bewildering kiss.

And so the games begin. Trent feints, Mazie parries. He threatens, she pretends nonchalance. He cajoles, she rebuffs. Thwarted at every turn, Trent probes deep into her one vulnerability—her past. There he finds the leverage he needs and a searing truth that challenges all he believes about right and wrong.

Warning: The delicious, if left-brained, hero might forever change all you think you know about the Robin Hood legend. Contains razor-sharp wordplay, skinny dipping and tortured hearts.

Available now in ebook and print from Samhain Publishing.

SAMHAIN
PUBLISHING

www.samhainpublishing.com

Green for the planet.
Great for your wallet.

SAMHAIN
PUBLISHING

It's all about the story...

Romance

HORROR

www.samhainpublishing.com

CPSIA information can be obtained at www.ICGtesting.com
Printed in the USA
LVOW061930180413

329843LV00012B/1101/P